Wayne Sharrocks was born in the London borough of Camden. After attending college, he embarked on a career within animal welfare before returning to his passion for writing.

He now lives in the picturesque village of Blo Norton in the heart of the Norfolk countryside and is enjoying his new profession as an author of psychological thrillers.

'Redemption' is his debut novel but there are two more books already in the pipeline for future release.

In his spare time he enjoys art & design and is still a keen supporter of a number of animal welfare charities.

REDEMPTION

Wayne Sharrocks

Redemption

Vanguard Press

VANGUARD PAPERBACK

© Copyright 2006
Wayne Sharrocks

A CIP catalogue record for this title is
available from the British Library

ISBN 1 84386 254 9

Vanguard Press is an imprint of
Pegasus Elliot MacKenzie Publishers Ltd.
www.pegasuspublishers.com

First Published in 2006

Vanguard Press
Sheraton House Castle Park
Cambridge England

Printed & Bound in Great Britain

Dedication

For Shaz...

My elegant enchantress, who brought light
where there was dark and hope where there was
despair...

PROLOGUE

The sunlight was just beginning to dim as I was led along the dark wooded pathway and through the endless tangle of trees and bushes. Overhanging branches and thorned shrubs snagged at my clothing as I walked. I inhaled slowly, deeply, taking in the day's remaining heat as a droplet of sweat broke free from my hairline. I now found myself surrounded on all sides by the gang whose cries both delicious and cruel, were suffused with the rich scent of doom and echoed through the woodland as we strode. As I stumbled forward, through the grove of trees, crackling leaves underfoot, a shiver shot straight through me and I felt distinct unease. I was finding it difficult to acclimatize to my new surroundings and was feeling distinctly unnerved by the gang's words which sounded like wolves howling in the night, their baying cacophony competing for space in my head. I felt decidedly uncomfortable and more than a little confused by the unfurling events.

Although more than two years younger I longed to be as one with them, one of the gang, as I was sick of being perceived as the school geek and a constant victim of their casual brutality. How I had yearned for their acceptance. I had prayed previously that this day would soon come, but now that it was finally upon me I felt distinct unease, even though I knew that all I needed to do now was to pass this initiation rite and my life would be changed forever. For the better... or so I hoped.

The thought fluttered through my mind as if caught on a breeze. The loathsome gang consisted of four main members, although others came and went at somewhat regular intervals. Steve was the gang's figurehead and my main tormentor. He was only fifteen but was already approaching six feet tall and had the physique of a middleweight boxer but unfortunately with the attitude and ill temper of a barroom brawler. All the local boys feared him, whilst all the local girls worshipped him... He revelled in their acclamation of him.

His three accomplices on this occasion were: James (his younger brother), Peter and John. Their parents apparently having had very apt foresight as they were obviously disciples by nature as well as in name.

They were a ragtag army; all attired in faded blue denim jeans, leather jackets and baseball boots. Their faces were glistening with sweat, whilst their dark coarse hair was wild and unkempt and if truth be known they looked like pubescent roadies for Status Quo.

To be honest I was surprised when they had asked me join their gang as they were boys who liked to indulge their baser desires and I had been the butt of their jokes and the target of their cruelty for as long as I could remember…"faggot", "queer", "poof"… their words and cruel taunts intermingled with the images of prior beatings at their hands and echoed chillingly inside my head as I walked.

My breath was rabid and laboured and my lungs blazed from the exertion, as I had always been a sickly child (you name the ailment and I had suffered from it).

As I burst through the undergrowth I felt a sudden chill as fear hit me but I tried my best to bite back the feeling, as I knew that I must not let them see that I was afraid… after all I was going to soon be one of them, part of their gang, their family.

I felt pursued by a pack of unanswered questions, even just walking I felt tense, especially when my gaze absently flicked down to the serrated grasses that slashed like knives at my ankles as I walked.

C'mon Jamie, you can do it, I silently urged myself, you have survived your father's lashings and your mother's vicious tongue so you can survive this.

As we burst through the bushes we came to a clearing, where I caught a glimpse of the entrance to the disused underground air raid bunker. My pace faltered as I longed to just turn on my heels and flee… no point though, I knew that, as they were all older, bigger, stronger and faster than I.

Sweat masked my face as images from the book, 'Lord of the Flies' kept flashing through my mind and did nothing to settle my nerves and fear. God, how I wished now that I had never studied it in school. I knew that there was no way for me to back out now and as I pushed a branch aside, rustling the bushes, I felt acid bubbling in my stomach, whilst my nerves were like a squirming tangle of snakes.

12

My heartbeat quickened and I was now aware that I was breathing hard as I heard desperate rasps of breath escape from me. I felt a tickle as a droplet of sweat slid down my back to be presumably soaked up by the waistband of my trousers.

"C'mon Jamie, stop falling behind, not chicken are you?" called Steve, in mocking tones. He stomped off, his laugh echoing through the woodland.

"N-n-no, of c-course not," I stammered back, although my stuttering had now obviously unveiled my true feelings to him. Damn…the words had jammed in my throat as, in my mind; the thoughts of impending doom had come to the fore.

"All you have to do is let us shut you in the bunker, on your own for an hour, to confirm your bravery to us. Then we will come back and let you out and you can be part of our gang. Nothing could be simpler. There is nothing to fear, we have all had to do it," came the retort. I could not fail to miss the scornful lilt in his voice.

"No problem." I cringed as I heard my voice rise, nearly shrill and inaudible, but I felt as though I'd had to say something in a vain attempt to mask my growing fear and trepidation. As I wiped the sweat from my face I heard myself swallow loudly and felt my lips moving soundlessly, uttering a silent prayer of hope. I knew that there was no time for lingering, so continuing with the (now somewhat ailing) show of fake bravado I reluctantly stepped forward towards the imposing entrance of the subterranean cavern with its impressively thick reinforced steel door and elongated handle. The door clearly had not been opened for a long time as its lock was scaly with rust. I silently prayed that the door would be immovable but I was to be disappointed as the door creaked faintly open.

A million thoughts were flashing through my mind, the foremost of which was why a twelve-year-old boy was allowing himself to be locked in a pitch black pit for an hour to be part of a gang whose members he secretly loathed, but by the time reason had beckoned it was all too late. I looked on in horror as the metal entrance cover was unlocked and tugged open. It was accompanied by baleful laughter, but I did not demur.

Had I been tricked? Were they going to leave me here? Was I going to die? The questions stabbed in my mind like daggers. I knew now how Caesar had felt.

The breathing darkness seemed to lurch towards me as my body flooded with trepidation and adrenaline, fear gripping me like a vice. I knew that it was too late for me to back out now so I tried to compose myself as best I could and began to try thinking more positively.

They would only be gone an hour. I would be alright. After all they had asked me to join their gang hadn't they, as a way of making it up to me for past bullying, and of course they had all gone through this before… hadn't they?

My gaze flicked down and reluctantly and nervously I stepped inside the bunker as the gang's heckling stung my ears. As I glanced around, I thought I saw a glimmer of cunning light their eyes, whilst I felt their hands pushing and shoving at my back, urging me to descend the wrought iron staircase. They saw the terror in my eyes and drank it in, but by now their deferential manner and their mocking tones and words were barely penetrating my reverie as my mind had protectively closed in around me.

The smell of the repellent bunker was acrid and musty with damp and I felt a waft of fetid air. I could hear water trickling down the walls, smell the damp moss on the stairwell and hear the scuttle of what sounded like millions of unseen insects on the floors and surfaces. Every nerve in my body screamed for me to just turn and run but I knew that it was far too late for that now.

My heart was now pounding so hard that I thought it may leave my chest completely and I felt that my palms were already growing slick from perspiration.

When I had reached the earthen floor at the bottom of the staircase I saw that it was covered in dead withered leaves and threadbare old blankets, which I noted, much to my horror, were swarming with colonies of ants and assorted bugs. A huge dead beetle lay in the centre of one of the blankets, like some bizarre New Age sculpture. I felt as though I had just stepped onto the set of a Hammer Horror movie and prayed that at any moment a director would yell 'cut'!

Fear reached down within my stomach and squeezed tightly as, over the fanfare of laughter from above, I heard the sound of the metal cover being slid back into place. The air thickened in front of me. I stood static, trembling as I thought that I saw something move from deep within the shadows and felt the blackness encroach upon me, freezing my joints and dimming my vision. I felt claustrophobic as the engulfing darkness descended upon me like a veil and sheer panic overwhelmed me instantly. I felt a shortness of breath and my nose and eyes were already experiencing discomfort from the cascading clouds of dust. I felt a draft as I moved and I felt cobwebs brush against my face. Blinking rapidly whilst struggling against the darkness my hands moved quickly to wipe them away. My skin crawled just to touch them and this only added to my distress as I could not abide spiders at the best of times and the thought of them even touching me immediately turned my blood to ice. The hair on my arms and at the base of my neck stood to attention. My previous show of fake bravado had now left me completely as years of pent up and agonized frustration erupted to the surface like a volcano of emotion.

Smothered in black, my distress was all too evident as I began to shake uncontrollably. Utterly terrified I screamed, howling at the top of my lungs to be set free as fear permeated from my every pore and turned my pulse to static. I waited for my eyes to readjust to the darkness as I felt as though the walls were closing in around me, suffocating me, as if absorbing my very soul. Panicking I reached out for the stair rails, only to feel an unpleasant slippery liquid substance upon them.

Grimacing with disgust at the slime and the dirt I screamed out again. Flinching and repulsed, I wiped my hand on my faded denim jeans. My mind was working furiously in an attempt to combat the fear and revulsion I felt. Carefully I began my ascent again, rising slowly, cautiously placing one training-shoed foot in front of the other before I committed my full weight upon it as I feared losing my footing and balance on the dark, damp and slippery staircase. I glanced down at my watch but it was too dark to see its face. I could see nothing, just pitch blackness and fear shrouded me again. I stood shaking, bit my lip and tasted blood as fear coursed through my veins. Seized by the sense of urgency I began hammering on the metal door, screaming at the top of my lungs to be set free.

My cries were so loud that my eardrums threatened to split.

My scream was full of agony and desolation and continued for as long and as loud as my lungs and voice could sustain it. The sound of my anguish and despair reverberated off the subterranean walls of the wretched bunker, echoing my frustrated desperation, amplified sounds of my own unbearable terror.

Surely they would not abandon me here, leaving me to meet my maker?

I pressed my ear to the metal seal but could hear nothing, aside from my rapid heartbeat pumping in my ears. Either the gang had now gone or they were successfully stifling their laughter. I stood there, legs trembling as I listened. I tried to spy a keyhole but found none, so I assumed that the keyhole cover had either slid back across the lock therefore masking it or Steve had blocked it up to cut out my only light source and intensify my distress.

With hindsight, it was probably the latter choice.

Grim faced I pounded my fist on to the door again until my knuckles bled, but I received no aid and the formidable barricade to my safety remained unmoved. I winced at the pain my foolish actions had caused me and I felt tortured by the vagrant currents of air coming through the locked and barricaded door. As things stood I had no way of gaining my freedom from within this dark and daunting chasm. I was trapped and now felt as if I had been dropped into the bowels of hell itself. The fact that this recent past would inevitably become a terrible future only served to increase my sense of sheer helplessness. Inside my head I heard myself scream again (with a combination of anger and fear) although I think this time no sound had actually left my lips. I chewed the skin around my thumb nails, eventually drawing blood, which I drank hungrily.

There was something comforting about the warm nectar that flowed from my digit as my mind raced plotting an escape from this landscape of despair. The frail blue flame of hope deep inside was waning as what seemed like hours passed. The oppressive atmosphere pressing down upon me, the damp and darkness suffocating me, my head spinning as I seemed to flit in and out of consciousness: I felt completely disorientated and claustrophobic, feeling as if I had been buried alive.

The thought was like ice in my stomach as the blood froze in my veins. By the minute my mood was ever darkening. The sudden silence was deafening and a shiver ran through me as the temperature had noticeably dropped. The dank chill and musty odour had now enveloped me totally and I just could not stop shivering. I loathed being cold so I began to frenetically rub my hands up and down my arms to try and generate some warmth.

My heart jumped as I was gripped by panic and lip quivering fear. Anxiety was stretching at my every fibre as I sensed that the gang were still out there beyond the locked and barricaded door... laughing at my expense no doubt, chortling at my abasement and humiliation. I felt totally degraded whilst my mind was plagued with doubt and insecurity.

Why were they keeping me waiting? Surely the hour must be up by now?

Cold and fear had engulfed me again (a combined embrace that threatened to drive me insane) whilst down below I heard the scuttle of unseen vermin which filled me with dread and loathing. I stared down into the darkness, in the direction of the scrabbling sounds but I could see nothing. I feared that it may be rats and I was instantly filled with repugnance and dread. I could almost sense their countless beady black eyes boring into me.

The sound appeared to be closing in on me as I stood frozen in terror upon the staircase. I prayed that it was just an acoustical trick of the bunker as revulsion had tightened my throat and a crawling sensation now spread across my skin. I could feel the onset of a terrible headache as my temple pulsated and my eyes stung. The air was dusty and acrid and I could feel it sear my lungs. These passing minutes seemed to be lasting a lifetime. I felt my heartbeat quicken as icy fear held me in a vice-like grip. I tried to urge myself to breathe deeply and to relax as I could feel myself beginning to hyperventilate. I felt as though I was being swallowed by the bunker's impenetrable darkness.

I was feeling tired and fraught and obviously becoming prey to my own fertile imagination. Tears combining fear and frustration were suddenly flowing down my cheeks as I knew that I had no option but to wait in the dark. I could taste every bitter salty tear and now I just wanted it all to stop.

For a long frozen moment time stood still. I could not move

and did not dare breathe as terror ripped through my bowels. I found myself sweating profusely but yet I was still shivering from the combination of cold and trepidation.

How I loathed the endless pockets of damp and darkness. It was pure torture.

The gang had played on my torment and brought me to my knees. I was still rigid with fear as my temple throbbed like a drum and my heart began to pound so hard that for an instant the world turned black. The darkness that had now engulfed me was all too complete as my now frantic screams rang and echoed through the bunker.

Again I thought that I could die here, in this acrid, dark, damp abominable hell of a place... No, my parents (if sober) would be worried, they would call the police, and they would ring the school. I would be found... I was sure.

I sat waiting in this abandoned subterranean bunker, immersed in darkness, the deafening silence only eventually being broken by the sound of my own pounding heartbeat and the scurrying atrocities below. I bit back a shriek as my stomach lurched and I vomited my lunch onto the bunker's floor. For several minutes I crouched there, unable to move as my stomach cramped. I took a deep breath, but the very taste of fear filled my mouth. As my horror rose I doubled over retching, lurching forward to spill whatever was left in my stomach. This time though it was just a thin stream of bile. I spat to clear the taste from my mouth, and then wiped my face with my tee-shirt as I took another deep breath of foul air...

Hours later, I sat huddled on the stairs in an almost foetal position, with my arms clamped tightly around my body for warmth, whimpering as agony and fright seeped from my every pore. The growing knot of despair tangled deep within me as a crawling sensation ran down my spine. I subconsciously began to regress and started rocking to and fro... as if I were a baby in a crib. I began to cradle myself in the belief that I was alone in a world bathed in darkness.

Fear paralysed me as if I were being held in an ice cold vice. Feeling desperate, I began humming and singing to myself in a vain attempt to while away the time and to try to belatedly inflate my flagging spirits. I sat huddled, but awake, desperately trying to fight off the unease that prevented me from closing my eyes. I had to believe that I would soon be free again and that my hunger, tiredness and raging thirst would then be appeased. Everything was going to be alright...

At some point I must have passed out as I awoke from my limbo of darkness to find the bunker door standing ajar and the sound of shrill squawks of laughter and gleeful asides assaulting my senses. Rays of sunlight bounced off the blackened walls. The howls of the gang's laughter were almost as loud as the screaming inside my head. I glanced down at my hands and saw that my palms were slippery from sweat and grease, whilst my nails were shattered and caked in dirt and blood. My back throbbed and ached as I unfolded painfully from squatting, but tension pulled me to my feet.

I noted that it was now daylight, and the realization that I had now been trapped here all night dawned upon me. I slumped with relief. My senses were being overloaded with a mixture of joy, relief, fear and foreboding. Joy and relief for my obvious release but fear and foreboding for the inevitable brutal punishment that awaited me at home for being out all night. I was trying to get my senses and feelings into some sort of context as, joints aching, I exited the shelter. I paused to try and compose myself as I ascended the bunker's short flight of stairs, as I felt my legs slightly buckle from under me and found that my vision was slightly blurred. It felt as though I were walking on a sheet of thin ice and I walked decidedly gingerly. I wearily rubbed the back of my aching legs as I had the shuffling gait of a geriatric, for the moment, debilitated by the stiffness of having spent a long fraught night curled up on the hard staircase (my lofty position of sanctuary from the terrifying scrabbling creatures below).

My joints and muscles cried out in anguish, my shoulder felt badly jarred and my neck as though it had suffered whiplash. I felt dizzy and confused, obviously brought on by my tiredness and pangs of hunger which stopped me from thinking clearly. My whole body shook and there was screaming inside my head and my soul, which felt fractured to the bone. Even though I was now released I felt as if I were still being driven mad with fear...

The barrage of laughter, mocking and teasing increased as,

averting my eyes, I stepped out into the light. The dazzling abrupt definition of sight hurt my eyes so I squinted and raised my hand in an attempt to shield my eyes from the sun (as they desperately tried to re-adjust themselves). I looked and felt as though I had just been vomited from hell itself.

I quickened my pace as the realization that it had all been a game to them and the knowledge that I was never going to be one of their gang hit me like a sledgehammer. I knew now that I had been through this entire nightmare for nothing ...

I would never fit in, I would never be like them... my slight build, effeminate manner, high pitched voice and feminine features would ensure that. I began to cry, I tried my best to stem the flow but the tears had already welled up and were now beginning to cascade down my cheeks before my bony hands had a chance to brush them away. My streaming eyes blinked at the faces bunched around me.

This was the 'cherry on the cake' as far as Steve and his cohorts were concerned as the jeers and howls of laughter intensified to a crescendo, relishing my fate. Their words seemed evilly gleeful and were cruel and cold and without mercy. Suddenly I felt too much alone, the pain becoming unbearable.

I winced and gritted my teeth as humiliation shot through me. I covered my ears to shut out the torment and looked away from the obvious glee that was now etched onto all of their faces (as they bore down on me like a pack of hyenas scenting blood).I realised that I would never receive any mercy from them and the atmosphere was now so intense and cloying that I felt physically sick.

I did not speak, choosing to remain silent but instead I just turned and ran through the haze that rippled around me, never once looking back. My heart was racing as I crashed through the undergrowth, not feeling the overhanging branches slashing at the bare skin on my face, neck and arms, nor hearing the baleful laughter echoing through the trees following me as I fled, mocking my every step. Branches whipped my face and body raising welts like the marks of a flagellant, whilst a solitary cry (that was beyond the anguish of words) echoed through my throat and through my mind. The moment seemed so unreal and so prolonged but I knew that the sting of humiliation would now be with me for eternity, with no way of it ever being reconciled.

It was one of the most painful and embarrassing moments of my relatively short young life. I had been mentally battered and broken. I knew from that moment that my life would never be the same again and that I could now never return home as the demons that were previously built almost entirely of myth, were now a very real childhood nightmare. I felt hollow and bruised, filled with regret and recriminations as I prayed aloud that the gods would numb my awareness and haze my pain. I knew that I would have to build a wall to keep the rest of the world out.

May the gods help me…?

CHAPTER 1

CONSCIENCE

I awoke trembling and sweating, the sheets soaking wet beneath me as my mind recalled the visions from the nightmare that had violently ripped me from my sleep. The recollections were sadly all too vivid as I had been fighting them all night, a battle I was destined to lose.

Damn, twenty years on and still the memory of those events would not fade. I felt the maelstrom of reproach and morbid regrets as every night seemed to rekindle old memories that I wished to leave behind and to deny the existence of. Sometimes I found myself closing my eyes and hiding away in the dark. I knew that there was a lot to be ashamed of in my life, but I just did not understand why these dark thoughts and spectres from my past, kept invading my mind of late, now almost on a nightly basis. I always felt exhausted upon waking due to the upsetting dreams and unwelcome presences disrupting my slumber and I was now sick of continually waking up in cold sweats. I had always hoped that my mind would bury the experience if my will was strong enough, but alas it was not to be, as the scar tissue had peeled away, leaving me raw.

My temple was beginning to throb so I rolled over in bed, opened my eyes and looked across into the semi darkness at the illuminated face of the now buzzing alarm clock, which sat perched precariously upon the bedside table. It was pleading for me to arise. I looked at it for a few seconds, whilst attempting to focus my eyes and clear my head, before turning off its infernal din. I reluctantly slipped out from beneath the covers and headed towards the bathroom. Pulling on the cord to the light, I then recoiled at the vision that confronted me from the bathroom mirror. The fact that I'd had a restless night was etched into every pore and crevice of my milk white skin. My eyes were bloodshot and drowned in themselves.

I looked like Bela Lugosi, which was not necessarily so bad in itself, except for that fact that he had been dead since 1956.I ran the taps, filling the wash basin, and splashed water onto my face in a vain effort to revive myself. My mouth was dry, filled with a sour taste, my teeth stained red. Was I drinking a Merlot last night? I could not recall... Why did I still keep having these memory lapses decades on, I silently asked myself as I patted my face dry with a hand towel. I wondered how I would make it through the day with so little sleep. As I spat toothpaste and saliva into the basin, I was still feeling slightly uneasy as my body felt bound with tension. I gargled with some foul tasting mouthwash before leaving the room and padding sleepily into the kitchen to fill the kettle for a much needed caffeine fix. The stale aroma of last night's takeaway still floated from the kitchen and pressed me for recollections that just would not come. I rubbed at my throbbing temple. I wanted my life back and I desperately needed comfort and solace and to move on with my life. I needed something tangible, as at present my thoughts were all too intrusive and upsetting. I was only too aware that time, brutality and distant nostalgia had hammered every trace of boyish innocence out of me and that I no longer looked at the world with an open mind. I knew that I had become an emotional heretic although I was not completely dissolute, or so I liked to believe.

I lit a cigarette and inhaled deeply on it in a bid to settle my nerves whilst I attempted to pull upon the invisible strings to my mind. I was tired and ached all over.

My concentration was suddenly exploded by the thundering of the letterbox as the daily paper, inevitably torn, thudded onto the doormat. I walked to the hallway and crouched down to pick it up. Unfolding it, as I glanced down, I was greeted by the headline 'LOCAL WOMAN FOUND STRANGLED'.

Once this was a nice safe neighbourhood but no longer. This was the third reported murder within the borough in less than a month so fear and anxiety in the community were understandably rife.

Women no longer ventured out alone and even men made lame excuses to have companionship should they need to venture out after dark. This latest revelation did little to settle the unease in my mind but my train of thought was suddenly broken as I heard the kettle switch itself off. Returning to the kitchen I made a mug of strong coffee, adding a tot of brandy for good measure. I still felt ill at ease even though the sofa, that I now occupied, was designed for maximum relaxation. I assumed that it was always better to be miserable in comfort, so my whole apartment, which consisted of lounge chairs, lush plants, plush furnishings and long glass cabinets containing crystals, semi-precious stones and rock strata was my futile and vain bid to bring a peaceful and ambient serenity to my troubled life.

Something was nagging at me but I could not explain where the feeling had come from or what it meant as my mood swings were fast becoming a turbulent roller coaster of emotions. My eyes drifted to the window as my mind flicked back to my childhood where I recalled the educational psychologist stating that I was socially dysfunctional, and desperately needed to develop social skills to enable me to interact successfully with other children. My teachers stating that I always had my head in the clouds…

My father's answer to those assessments was to unstrap his thick belt and lash me with it, as if this was a sure-fire way to instil discipline into me. The fact that it had not worked for the previous eleven years did not seem to overly phase him. Feeling the tears starting in my eyes I shuddered and blinking shook the image from my mind. I pulled open the curtains and focused out of the window, noticing that the soft pale blue sky was almost cloudless. The shrubbery outside was a wonderful collage of green shades, the vision only spoilt briefly by an empty discarded crisp packet that was tumbling acrobatically in the breeze.

I arose from the comfort of my seat and walked back to the bathroom to get showered and dressed, determined to enjoy the beautiful summer's day. Once I was showered and crisply attired perhaps I would take my paintbrushes, oils, pastels and charcoal and capture the beauty of nature's elements as I painted best when under stress and had several hours to kill before the weekly appointment with my analyst. I usually found both events very relaxing and meditative... a therapeutic way of releasing the burdens of the day and to feel at peace.

I had plenty of free time on my hands now, since a couple of months ago I had been given a substantial severance payment from Hemscott investment brokers, my previous employers. I had been off work for four months previously, with what my doctor described as 'severe depression, emotional stress and mental strain', but then anyone would be a bit down after their partner ended a ten year marriage, bled their bank account dry and ran off with their best friend, would they not?

OK, so I thought she loved me but I now knew that was all a lie. Everything. The whole relationship was a complete sham from start to finish. I had just been used for the financial security and I knew now that I had never satisfied her. I felt the agony of unbelievable loss and grief as unfortunately even an acrimonious ending to a relationship does not end the feelings.

I knew that I had lost her; she was gone and would not be coming back. I only wished that I could leave my bleeding heart behind as my wife had caused me irreparable emotional damage, eating away at me like a parasite, but I suppose we all have our own hidden agendas? What was the old adage? ...you fall in love and fall in debt. Perhaps there was some truth in that as there is always a different face but the words never change.

I knew that there was no magic formula for the happiness and the solace which would then enable me to move on with my life. At this thought an immeasurable sense of loss settled over me. Everything that I had cherished in life had been torn from me and at the time I could not think of a single reason to go on. My entire life had gone up in smoke, my career, my marriage and now possibly my future. I knew that I could never trust anyone again. No-one had ever believed in me and the thought of eventually proving them wrong was currently the only consideration keeping me alive. I just had to hope that with every passing day my mind would grow easier.

I had accrued a great many chips on my shoulder over the years but who would have thought that I would have been betrayed by the only person that I had ever trusted or that love could have cut so deep? Much like with the salmon, sex proved to be the ultimate killer.

I felt myself convulse and shiver as the sensation of desolation rose within me.

The heart that she had left behind was broken and I was left utterly shattered. The depth of my grief had shocked even me as I had not realised quite how much I had loved her. I thought that I might never recover from the loss, as I now had proof positive that love and hate were just the same: one emotion, just a different name.

God, I missed her like crazy... but I still wished that she were dead.

CHAPTER 2

ENTICEMENT

The ongoing counselling that I was undertaking, I felt, had been of some benefit and I was determined to approach this new period of my life in a more positive manner.

After all if you do not live for something you die for nothing. I felt the first stirrings of confidence. Everything was going to be alright. The pack of demons had been vanquished (for the moment) and a cosy veil of thought ripped through my mind. My game plan was to finally meet my soul mate/kindred spirit. I was still young (ish), financially secure (for the moment) and reasonably attractive so surely there was someone out there who would want to share life's journey with me and to cherish, love and adore me? My counselling session had left me with this new found objective and having since exercised my artistic talents earlier today, (creating a glorious watercolour on Montval paper of a view within London's Hyde Park), I felt refreshed, tranquil and motivated. I had successfully fought off this morning's demons.

Transacted by the sunlight cascading down in between the huge stores, I found myself walking down Oxford Street, and fighting for elbow room with the tourists, the off-from-work-early crowd, the great unwashed and the beggars that lined the pavements, bedecked in blankets that failed to obscure their top of the range training shoes and accompanied by their seemingly compulsory tools of the trade, the obligatory cardboard sign (with atrocious spelling) and undernourished stolen dog on a bit of rope. I was not sure that was quite what Margaret Thatcher had in mind when she urged free enterprise back in the 1980s though.

The stalls, hawkers, cafes, pubs, stores and restaurants all seemed to be doing a roaring trade under the cloudless cobalt sky, obviously buoyed by the surprisingly (for England) mild clement weather. Despite the usual gridlocked traffic, there was a definite buzz in the air. As I would obviously not be getting anywhere fast by either bus or taxi cab I decided upon a drink and so headed towards the Marlborough Head Tavern, which was just off of Bond Street, as it appeared to be the nearest public house with which I was familiar.

Entering the establishment I turned left and continued downstairs to the basement bar where the lighting and ambience I knew from previous experience to be more subdued.

Stepping up to the bar I was greeted in soft Scandinavian tones from the vision behind the counter. I ordered a brandy and coke on the rocks and perched upon the barstool, exchanging flirtatious banter with the barmaid until she was called away to serve another patron. Just my luck.

I reached into my jacket pocket for my cigarettes and lighter. I took a cigarette from the packet and lit it with the plastic disposable lighter (with a playboy bunny motif) which I then returned to my pocket. I exhaled smoke towards the ceiling and then found myself temporarily partially obscured by the thin veil of smoke that had fallen over me, as if a dissipating halo. Very apt I thought, given my life.

I heard myself unconsciously sigh with loneliness, so risking the pain of rejection I scanned the establishment for some female action, but just the usual regulars and girls who looked young enough to be my daughters were seated in the downstairs area. I caught my reflection in the mirror behind the bar, maybe it was just the flattering lighting, but the vision that stared back at me was not at all shabby. My autumnal long mane full of body and shine, my features delicate and pretty rather than handsome and my lithe frame crisply attired in a long black velvet jacket and white cotton shirt. I could now see what made me such a prized catch during my rent boy days.

The recollection now repulsed me, but although not gay by nature, a runaway twelve year old had very few employment options. I was young, naive and malleable. At the time I was a heartbreaking mixture of helplessness and vulnerability but I had eventually learnt to let my mind leave my body whilst the vile repulsive acts were being administered or received. My vulnerability had soon been spotted and breached as I had attempted to adapt to my new surroundings... the city that was supposedly paved with gold, but in truth I found to be paved with drugs, lies, vice and unwavering misery. Not forgetting the numerous 'care' homes from which I absconded at somewhat regular intervals, as at least out on the streets I was paid for the sex and it was not seen as a perk of the job. I ground my teeth in self-disgust and self-loathing as I slumped inside myself.

Some thoughts and memories can be deeply shameful and unbelievably destructive. Thankfully my train of thought was suddenly broken as I noticed a flash of movement on the stairs towards the entrance of the bar. A woman, probably in her mid to late twenties, maximum early thirties, had just swept in. She had the face of an angel and was impossibly beautiful. Her skin was the colour of alabaster and her lips were full and red. She wore a simple but sexy white knee-length summer dress, with a split up one side that accentuated her pleasingly slim figure and her shapely calves. She wore a delicate ankle chain and a silver chain around her neck that was slightly obscured by her cascading golden mane. Her almost feline teal eyes briefly met mine as she sidled towards the bar, pulled out a stool and ordered a dry white wine. I noted that she had no ring on her wedding finger. Things had just looked up and the gods were obviously smiling upon me.

I think in awe of her beauty that my mouth had even fallen open a little as I attempted to casually reach down for my drink. In need of stimulus and support I took a sip and sighed contentedly with relief as the warmth and the thrill of it slid down my throat. My heart raced a little faster as I took another sip and stirred the ice in the glass. The rattling sound had the desired effect and the angel in my midst glanced over in my direction. I studied her expression as our eyes met and I smiled. Fortunately for me she maintained eye contact and reciprocated with a radiant smile, her incredibly green eyes warm and welcoming. I felt a glimmer of excitement as I immediately felt an affinity with her…

She looked as pure as driven snow… I just hoped that looks were deceiving. I felt cautious anticipation, as my heart thudded, tripping with nervous excitement.

The game had begun…

I took another glance and noticed her green-blue eyes, noted the warmth in them and felt instantly at ease. I ordered another brandy and coke with ice for me and another white wine for the vision seated beside me. As I placed the Chablis in front of her, she thanked me with a smile. I took a healthy sip of my brandy, feeling its warmth and felt it already beginning to relax me. My smile was gentle and friendly although inside I longed to hold, hug and caress her, to bond in both an emotional and physical sense. I had never believed in love at first sight before this moment but now I was totally besotted. She was just so exquisite that I longed to make her mine.

Again her eyes met mine, but this time just staring. She was not smiling, but there was, what looked like, humour in her eyes. I hoped that she wasn't secretly deriding me, but then she did smile and its warmth and genuineness was all-consuming. After this initial awkwardness and the obligatory formal introductions we ended up chatting for hours, the connection and attraction instant on both our parts. The sound of her laughter held such an exotic charm for me as her voice was like pure silk and it made my heart race with excitement and anticipation. She had touched my erotic core and I felt sure that the sparks would soon begin to fly...

As we were both decidedly ravenous we decided to head off to the Sarastro restaurant, near Covent Garden, which was a slightly quirky place in the heart of London's theatre land.

We stepped out of the Marlborough Head public house and into the night air which was cool and moonlit. God, I could not believe how quickly the time had flown. We had chatted unabated for hours, like a pair of star crossed lovers (or so I liked to think... although the truth was that it was probably more akin to a couple of old fishwives).

The temperature had definitely fallen, the wind picking up with the breeze ruffling our hair as we strolled. After a few minutes of walking down Bond Street, unsuccessfully trying to flag down a black cab, an unlicensed taxi swung to a halt beside us. We climbed in and we were soon weaving our way through the London traffic and past the traffic lights blinking emptily towards Kemble Street, which was just off of Drury Lane.

The cab driver was an odd chap with bizarre white facial hair which made him bear more than a passing resemblance to Papa Smurf. He had obviously grown the outlandish whiskers in a vain bid to compensate for his rapidly balding pate.

It was not a good move.

He seemed to have a view on everything from immigrants to law and order to where the English sporting teams were failing. Quite why he was not running the country was a mystery.

While he put the world to rights Nikki and I just stared distractedly out of the window, wishing the time away. To make matters worse, if that was possible, he insisted on playing some bizarre Irish/ folk/country hybrid cassette. It sounded like the result of some bizarre cloning experiment between Daniel O' Donnell, Billy Ray Cyrus and a cat in the throes of being neutered, all of which were far from an appetising combination, so I longed for the journey to end soon or for the tape to get chewed up… whichever came first would be fine with me.

Thankfully there was a God, and we arrived at our intended destination a short time later. With a sigh of relief, I noted that the theatre crowds were yet to depart from their respective shows, which was great, as that meant there should be some free tables in the restaurant. With hindsight I should have rung from the public house to pre-book but I felt that now we were here that we would be able to wing it.

I handed the taxi driver a ten pound note, told him to keep the change and swung open the cab door. A slow grin lit his eyes as I stepped out onto the pavement, taking care to sidestep a pigeon nodding to crumbs on the pavement. Once we were both safely ensconced on the pavement he accelerated away, cutting sharply in front of another unlicensed taxi, whose Asian driver leant on his horn indignantly and then proceeded to tailgate him down the road. Oh the cowboys of the road…it's all fun and games.

We crossed over the road and entered the restaurant whereupon we were greeted by what looked like a human penguin, but that in fact turned out to be a smiling waiter attired in black trousers, bow tie and waistcoat with his white shirt adding the only splash of colour to his ensemble. He had short raven black hair gelled back and the darkest eyes I had ever seen, almost akin to that of a seal.

"Would you have a table for two available?" I enquired.

"Certainly Sir, if you would like to follow me."

We did, but not that we really had any choice as he was the only one who knew where we were going...

The restaurant was as full of polite hushed tones as a library study area, whilst a thin blanket of piped music floated across the air, elusive as haze.

We were led to a discreet corner table set in a little alcove. It was the perfect romantic setting and I was delighted. The restaurant, even with its now subdued lighting was still incredibly rich in colour and texture with the furnishings and linen tablecloths offering garish splashes of colour against the restaurant's decorative and theatrical wooden surround.

As we took our seats I looked across into Nikki's eyes and noticed the smile that sparkled within them. She looked timidly mischievous and I was immediately engulfed by the combination of love, lust and desire that washed over me. Although I had not known her for very long my heart was literally ablaze and my soul on fire.

Her face was just so serene, her eyes warm and loving, whilst her full lips were ruddy with glee. She was just so beautiful and totally exquisite. I felt so proud to be seen with her and could not believe that such an angel was with me. To the waiter we must have seemed like beauty and the beast. It all seemed like a dream with half of me believing that this was all way too good to be true and that I would undoubtedly awaken at any moment.

Just then the waiter reappeared, as if the shopkeeper in the old Mr Benn television series, and produced two menus that were handed to us in turn. He then left us to consider our options. Nikki glanced up from her menu.

"As you know this place better than I, would you like to order for the two of us?"

Damn, the very question that I had been dreading as I was no wine connoisseur and knew that I would probably order the wrong wine to complement the meal. Perhaps I should play it safe and order a good champagne? Or would that come across as being too flash or presumptuous?

God, you didn't have any of this palaver at Burger King.

After changing my food/wine/champagne order over half a

dozen times in my mind I eventually decided to order us the avocado with prawns for starter, followed by stir fried breast of chicken with vegetables julienne. To accompany it I ordered a bottle of champagne Mumm Cordon Rouge.

I did not know how much of a terrible faux pas I had made or whether I had got away with my culinary naivety undetected. Not that I particularly cared once the food and drink arrived as the champagne turned out to be delightful. It was very fruity with an aroma of what seemed like grapefruit, peach and apricot type fruits. The meals when they arrived were delicious also, the chicken succulent and the vegetables crisp and fresh.

Nikki was an exquisite dinner date. She was truly a goddess in mortal form, an enchantress who left me enthralled and spellbound. The emotions and sensations that I had bubbling within were all very new to me and I wished now that this night would last forever…

Throughout the meal Nikki was just so attentive and amusing. She had such captivating charm and we found that we were so connected on so many levels that the conversation flowed easily between us. It was almost like fate had brought us together.

It felt like Kismet, and I found myself forever gazing at her face to delight in her beauty. She was beautiful both on the inside and out and looked positively radiant in the flickering candlelight. I felt utterly bewitched…

We finished off our meals with fresh fruit and coffees before departing into the cold night air. I waived the offer to 'Go Dutch' and left a substantial tip as I did not want to appear cheap in front of Nikki. Not that I felt the waiter deserved the tip mind you as he was buzzing around our table for most of the night like a bee with a stick up his arse.

Why are you no longer left alone to eat in peace when you visit restaurants, I pondered inwardly, it never used to be like this… did it?

My wandering thoughts were waylaid as Nikki slid her arm into mine as we walked out of the restaurant and into the cool night air. A gentle warmth ran through my body as she touched me. Nikki's arms were a warm sanctuary from the slight chill of the evening and the previous coldness of my life.

We momentarily stopped walking and looked up at the sky as the moon shone full and bright. The moonlit sky seemed so romantic somehow and Nikki slipped her arms around my neck and pulled me closer to her. She pressed her lips to mine, her tongue pushing through mine as my hands dropped from around her waist to gently caress her shapely bottom.

The crowds were now pouring out from the adjoining theatres and taking great interest in our primitive mating ritual, so giggling we broke our clinch and continued strolling down the road (past the vandalised telephone kiosks and intermittent lampposts), towards Oxford Street, stopping every so often to once again embrace and kiss. I felt Nikki beginning to feel colder so I slipped off my velvet jacket and draped it over her bare shoulders.

I felt as if I were a courting teenager again.

"Would you like to come back for a coffee?"

Her face was all open innocence but I could not fail to miss the real meaning for the invitation.

How could I possibly refuse?

I hurriedly hailed a cab. As we stepped inside and settled upon the back seat I knew that this would be a night I would remember forever. I just silently prayed that our new union would not be ephemeral...

When we saw the driver it was a mixed blessing. Thankfully for us it was not the same one that had driven us to the restaurant but this new one only spoke pidgin English and appeared not to know half the places in Central London. Fortunately he possessed a London A-Z, so Nikki carefully and painstakingly showed him what I presumed to be the quickest route, via Euston, Regent's Park and Baker Street.

He listened patiently, but in truth he was not the brightest lamp in the store, so I think that he would have been better off hopping out and letting one of us take the wheel instead.

Why is it that people with no local geographical knowledge or common sense (and would be politicians) all decide to become taxi drivers? I pondered if there was perhaps some secret clan of career advisors out there who were surreptitiously having an enormous belly laugh at our expense?

Our new taxi driver was as equally incredible looking as

our previous chauffeur. He was a very dark skinned guy with strangely braided wild hair that made him look like Medusa. He was attired in one of the most garish tropical shirts I had seen since the heydays of 'Black Lace' back in the 1980s.

Damn… I knew that I was not going to get 'Agadoo' out of my head all night now.

I surmised that either he was moonlighting as a Caribbean tourist advisor or he had recently hired Timmy Mallett as his tailor.

Neither were wise decisions…

I reached into my jacket pocket, now that Nikki had returned it to me in the cab, and withdrew my packet of cigarettes and lighter. I offered Nikki one, which she politely declined. As I tapped a cigarette out of the pack and placed it into my mouth to light it the driver grunted something in broken English, whilst gesticulating to a small 'no smoking' symbol on his dashboard.

Although I had stupidly left my Swahili-English phrasebook at home, I got the message.

Damn, I would now have to wait until we arrived at Nikki's abode to be able to smoke. I was feeling slightly nervous and sucking on a cigarette would have relaxed me nicely.

I glanced at my watch and noted that it was fast approaching the bewitching hour. Thankfully though I tended not to turn into a pumpkin, as the roads were still quite congested for this time of the night. I glanced out of the window at the cars forming long sinewy lines that from the sky must have looked like metal snakes. Not that I had ever seen a metal snake of course…

Note to self: Must get out more and stop watching 'Robot Wars'.

Nikki nestled up to me and rested her head on my shoulder whilst one of her hands held mine. The other one drifted onto my lap and after a while began casually stroking my inner thigh, occasionally brushing across my now fully erect penis. I wasn't sure whether to feel embarrassed as we had yet to be intimate or elated as I had promptly risen to the occasion at the slightest of provocation. I knew now that her love tonight was mine and with hindsight perhaps I had known this from the moment I first looked into her eyes.

I wondered if women experienced the same trials and tribulations regarding the mating ritual as men. If only there were policy guidelines, set in stone, it would make things so much easier all round, instead of this current 'trial and error' way of operating.

It was a pity that the gods had not been more pragmatic.

I mulled over that thought as we motored quietly, gliding past Baker Street tube station.

Nikki's body next to mine just felt so lovely and so right. My skin positively tingled at her touch whilst the scent of her perfume filled the taxi with a warm feminine fragrance of exotic floral, mandarin and coriander, truly the scent of an angel.

I would have to remember to sneak a look at the bottle to see which was her perfume of choice but knowing my luck it would be a top of the range designer make and I would have to take out a second mortgage to purchase a bottle of it. C'est la vie.

This just felt so loving and so right, us entwined together on the back seat. I noted that I was becoming increasingly aroused as Nikki's hand glided seamlessly over my body. I felt engulfed by the heat of desire that surged through me as if millions of tiny electric shocks were arcing my body, my hunger ignited.

My mind had become so distracted that I had failed to note just how far we had now gone on our journey, so I was taken by surprise as the cab pulled up to the kerbside and the gorgon I think stated words to the effect that we had arrived at our intended location.

Nikki slowly lifted her head from my shoulder and looked deeply and lovingly into my eyes before leaning forward to kiss me lightly and tenderly on the lips. After our brief exchange we swung the doors open and I reached into my leather wallet for a £20 note. I informed the driver to keep the change and as I climbed out from the backseat, he gave an affected smile and I think that he may have even grunted some form of thanks, but in all honesty it was very difficult to tell.

As I set foot on the pavement I glanced up to see that Nikki was already at the gate of her property. As her porch light shone brightly I could see that it was a lovely little 1840s terraced house with the exterior painted entirely white.

Very tranquil and quaint, I mused.

She smiled and as I walked towards her she thanked me for the meal and for what had so far been a lovely evening. The gleam in her eyes seemed dangerously eager as she reached for my hand. Now grasping it tightly, she led me up the garden path to her welcoming abode.

I slipped my arm around her waist as she fumbled in her handbag for the front door keys (typical woman, had everything in her handbag bar the kitchen sink). Upon eventually finding the key fob (which appeared to have a small troll on it that resembled me first thing in the morning) Nikki inserted the key into the lock and upon turning it, the door sprang open. I think both of us were relieved to get inside out of the cool night air and prowling wind that had been nuzzling at our faces.

As Nikki turned to close the door behind us I slipped my arms around her waist and pulled her closer to me, losing myself in the warmth she projected. Our lips met, tongues exploring each others mouths. She had teeth like pearls. I had never experienced such intense pleasure from just kissing before as kissing my wife had been like kissing a wet fish... and that was being kind. A romantic she was not. Well not with me anyhow, although my ex best friend may have been able to state somewhat differently. I shook the latter thought from my mind as I ran my hands through Nikki's luxuriously soft and silky hair and across her cheek before moving them gently and gracefully down over her breasts and back down to her waist. She was doing likewise to me, almost subconsciously mirroring my every move. She left a warm trail of desire wherever her hands explored and I hoped that I was doing likewise to her.

Nikki reached up to my shoulders and slid my jacket off, whereupon she began to unbutton my shirt which she then hurled away as passion was obviously overtaking her as well as me. Nikki's long cascading hair brushed my now naked torso as she butterfly kissed my neck and shoulders, nibbling gently on the now exposed flesh. I let out a low moan of ecstasy as intense delight spread through my entire body. As Nikki was already jacketless I reached behind her and delicately unzipped her dress, letting it fall on to the carpeted floor where we stood. The vision that confronted me was nothing short of heavenly (if ever an angel were to fall from heaven I felt sure that they would look like Nikki). She wore a white stretch lace bikini bra set that set my pulse racing and accentuated her perfectly tanned and toned body to perfection. A brief moment of panic went through me as I tried to recall what underwear I had on, but then I remembered that thankfully I had chosen to wear my black Thai silk boxer shorts today. I exhaled a sigh of relief as holey greying Y-Fronts tended to be a tad of a passion killer, as I bitterly knew from past experience...

With my mouth still fastened to Nikki's lips I unhooked the clasp of her bra strap and let it fall, allowing her soft pert milky white breasts to spring free. Glancing down I was relieved to note that they were perfect, as with the invention of the Wonder Bra you were never quite sure what you would be left with after said item was removed. I think that was why it was named the Wonder Bra; you remove it and then wonder quite where the cleavage went. Nikki's lips were still pressing on mine as her tongue explored my mouth whilst my fingers were running lightly over each of her breasts, tracing tiny circles over each erect nipple. Nikki let out a low moan of pleasure as I did so, obviously appreciative of the attention that she was receiving. I broke my lips from Nikki's and began to nibble on her earlobe and then blowing gently into her ear. I gradually worked my way down her neck and shoulders, kissing and biting lightly, which I could tell was exciting her as she was beginning to purr like a cat. My lips sank to the valley between her gorgeous breasts from where I kissed each in turn before sucking on her now hard and erect nipples, before rolling them around my tongue and nipping them gently. Her hands had since snaked between my legs caressing my pulsating throbbing rod and inner thighs. With a small cry, she threw her head back and arched her back. As her body trembled I could feel the waves of ecstasy washing over her, as well as myself. We sank on to the deep pile carpet, our bodies entwined together as if we were melting candles. Her limbs felt as smooth as ivory. Nikki grabbed my belt and proceeded to unfasten it before turning her attention to my zip. She slid it down and began to caress my now extremely erect and pulsating rod through the silky material of my boxer shorts.

She then removed her hand and all but ripped my trousers from me. I did likewise with her lace panties. The niceties were dispensed with (as the lust and passion were now all too consuming for the both of us), and we writhed entwined on top of the soft lush ochre carpet. I parted her bare soft silky legs and entered her heavenly gates, tasting her sweet juices as she bucked her hips into me, urging my tongue to explore her deeper. The pleasure increasing by the second as I tasted her sweet nectar. Nikki's soft sensual moans were ever exciting my senses and desire as (like with all men) I appreciated women who were noisy during love making.

After I had felt and heard the orgasm sweep through her body I rose up and slipped my rod deep inside her now moist and pulsating lips. Spasms of intense pleasure shot through my entire body as I did so. As I thrust into her with slow rhythmic strokes we kissed passionately, hungrily... our minds, body and spirit now as one. Nikki was just so passionate, sexy and sensual as she brought wave upon wave of pleasure coursing through my entire body. When eventually our bodies reached climax I felt as if my body might melt from the fire of passion that burned within me.

I wanted her. I loved her.

After thirty two years of pain and heartbreak I had finally experienced something real and tangible. The true meaning of life. Nikki was everything I had ever wished for and desired.

As a wave of humid heat washed over me, we lay silently entwined, our hearts beating together and I prayed that this would truly be a union that would last forever...

CHAPTER 3

THE NEXT DAY

I awoke the next morning bleary eyed and in a seemingly unfamiliar bedroom. Sleep had fallen away from me as if a thin veil that had now been lifted from my eyes. I could hear the roar of traffic outside the window and the sun was streaming in through the open curtains trapping sparkling particles of dust, whilst the sky outside looked as blue as an ocean, with yesterday's wind entirely gone. After focusing my eyes fully I was greeted by an array of wine bottles, ashtrays and a tabby cat (the latter of whom I have never been a great fan) curled up on a heavily cushioned chair opposite the bed, and who was currently giving me the evil eye.

Just what was it with women, cats and cushions? They somehow all seemed inextricably linked.

I looked across the bed and saw Nikki; my god I think that was her name, asleep on some large white fluffy pillows. Some recollection of the previous night of passion came drifting back to me, but I could not for the life of me remember what part of London I was now in, supposing of course that it was still London.

I eased myself gently out of the bed, sliding my legs down and perched on the edge of the mattress. I heard the bed springs creak softly as I stood up but fortunately Nikki remained undisturbed. I scanned the room but was unable to see my clothes, so to protect my modesty I grabbed the purple cowl neck chenille dressing gown hanging up on the door and went off in search of the bathroom. Luckily it was the next room so I flicked on the bathroom light and examined my tousled mane and lipstick-stained face in the mirror. I looked as though I'd had a great night even if most of it was now just a blur. I filled the basin and washed my face and body as best I could as I was not wanting to risk waking my new found angel by running a bath or shower just yet. I would ask her if I could use them later, once she had woken up. I was a bit unsure as to my next course of action, should I wake her, should I stay here in the apartment until she wakes or should I just slip out quietly and leave a note on the side? That was the trouble with being married for so long; you forgot the rules of dating. Not that I was a past master of dating etiquette pre-marriage you understand. I think the person who said 'Men are from Mars and Women are from Venus' hit the nail on the head perfectly, as in my experience women had their own set of rules and just when you thought you had them mastered they completely rewrote them.

Thankfully just as I was contemplating my options, and if the truth be known on the verge of tossing a coin to decide, Nikki appeared in the doorway, looking slightly dishevelled and gothic with smudged eyeliner and lipstick, but still undeniably beautiful and sensual. She was clad in a sheer silk scarlet teddy which instantly stirred erotic feelings within me.

She could not have offered a more tempting lure and it was a temptation that I could not resist.

Her eyes widened in surprise before we both smiled, and what could have been an awkward moment evaporated as she surveyed me standing there clad in her dressing gown. I started to say something, to explain, but then stopped, inhaling sharply.

Fortunately, both my heart and embarrassment soon melted though as Nikki let out a soft laugh before taking me in her arms and kissing me. Heaven was truly in her lips as I could not remember being kissed like that in a very, very long time. The passionate embrace was soft and sensual, but inside my heart was beating like a sledgehammer. I felt exhilarated. Could I have finally met someone who would love, cherish and emotionally support me?

Nikki led me back to her bedroom and we made love again. It was like fireworks going off on the fifth of November. I had never experienced such passion, fire and intensity in lovemaking before. Nikki looked gorgeous, her eyes sparkling with life and passion. She nuzzled into my ear as she led me back to her bed, her sensual body rubbing against mine as if a wildcat marking its territory. We kissed and she took my hand and led it down between her legs. She pulled me towards her and we kissed long and hard, biting each others' lips, sucking each others' tongues as lust flared. My whole body and soul swelled and shook with

desire as I caressed her pert breasts, running my hands over her
nipples that were now large and firm, and longing to be sucked. I
was only too happy to oblige as Nikki ran her fingers through
my mane. I went down lower, parting her legs, exposing her
pretty pussy lips. She knew what I wanted to do and lifted her
left leg over my shoulder as my tongue dived into her sweet
tasting honey pot. She was already quite wet with excitement
and this allowed me to slide my index finger inside her as I
began to lap at her sweet tasting nectar. I started with slow,
confident strokes then followed with fast little flicks on her
small bud. This continued for quite a few minutes as she
moaned, sighing loudly as she began to buck her hips, thrusting
her pussy further and deeper into my face. I continued lapping
hungrily until Nikki reached orgasm and a trickle of love juice
ran down her thigh, which I lapped up greedily. Nikki gave me a
contented and satisfied smile before pushing me down onto my
back. She fell down on top of me, kissing me deeply,
passionately, sucking and tasting her own juices in my mouth.
She then took the full length of me in her mouth, running her
teeth along the stem, hands cupping me. She continued for a
while but not wanting me to reach climax until I was inside her.

I closed my eyes and let the pleasure wash over me as she
then straddled my body, her tight pussy lips encasing my now
throbbing rod. She slowly lowered herself onto me, and the
feeling was incredible as she thrust down upon me. Her lips
brushed my ear, before proceeding to nibble at my lobe and
neck, as she gyrated above me. My hands grabbed her bottom as
she began to ride me harder, her body pressing against mine. She
leant forward so that I could roll her nipples in between my teeth
and lips. I could not last much longer as I thrust into her and I
began to moan as I felt my orgasm rising. For those moments I
was trapped in my idea of heaven and was oblivious to anything
else.

I was in a daze of sexual delight as wave upon wave of pure
pleasure soared through me and my body felt alive with new
previously untapped sensations. My heart pounded, my pulse
soared and my body shuddered with intense carnal pleasure,
luxuriating in the sensation. Nikki was wonderful, beautiful and
incredibly sexy and I longed for us to be more than passing ships

in the night. This was someone I wanted to love, cherish and protect ...forever.

Unfortunately for me Nikki had to work later that day (I found out that she managed a hair & beauty salon in London's West End) so a couple of hours later we embraced and kissed goodbye as I left her to get ready, promising to telephone her later that evening. As I departed Nikki's flat, daylight pricked my eyes like needles. The pale sunlight warming me as I breathed in the early morning air. Upon making my way home I found myself following a long gravel pathway, dappled in sunshine and decorated on either side by flower beds. I could hear the sound of my feet slowly crunching over the gravel as I walked. The scent of the freshly cut grass, mingled with the scent of the flowers temporarily masked the smell of the nearby take-away restaurants and the noxious petrol fumes, that unfortunately seemed to be synonymous with London these days.

It turned out that Nikki's house was in Notting Hill Gate, so as the weather was still dry and mild I decided to walk down to peruse the Portobello Road Market (as I had not frequented there in quite some time) and which was one of the few remaining places in London that boasted an authentic pie and mash shop. This had been my staple diet upon arriving in London at the tender age of twelve, courtesy of a lorry driver with a penchant for young boys.

I had not eaten today as yet, so being back in once all too familiar territory and never being one for fancy food, except when I was trying to impress on a date, I decided to make my way to the aforementioned shop. When I arrived, I discovered that it was under new ownership; a couple of women in their thirties, but the pie, mash and liquor sauce were as tasty, filling and cheap as ever.

My hand slid into my jacket pocket to reassure myself that the Post-it note with Nikki's telephone number on it was still present. It was and I relaxed. I could not believe that I had only met her yesterday as the conversation had flowed unabated and we had the closeness of people who had known each other for a lifetime.

Perhaps in a past life?

It was a real shame that Nikki had to go to work today, had clients booked in apparently, but hopefully this would be the start of something special and the new beginning that I had (for a long time) been so desperately seeking. Other women I had known paled in comparison and to have a future with someone who loved and cared for me and wished to spend the rest of their life with me was all that I had ever really desired. Who would have thought that for all these years it would prove so elusive?

I stared inquisitively out of the window, watching the general public scurrying around like worker ants, not once stopping to look and appreciate the surrounding beauty, to soak up the atmosphere or to absorb the melting pot of cultures around them. How much they were missing.

I glanced at my watch, longing for the evening to fall, so that I could telephone Nikki and once again hear her laughter and drink in her soft silky honey-coated voice. I experienced a light feeling in my chest and a quickening of my pulse at the thought of her. She had obviously awoken feelings that I thought had long since gone forever. It was a pleasant sensation and it felt good to have them now thoroughly reawakened.

Perhaps I should get her a little present, just a token gift?

I was sure that it would be viewed as a thoughtful gesture, so I would need to look around the antique and jewellery stalls for a beautiful, delicate and quaint item that perfectly reflected Nikki's persona. I suppose failing that I could always fall back on the old cliché of flowers and chocolates... Although I was far from a great fan of those, as they required little or no thought and tended to be the jurisdiction of cheating husbands who softened up their wives with those items, whilst behind their backs they shagged their secretaries. How bitter and cynical I had become.

I continued staring out of the café window, analysing people as they walked by, trying to guess their lifestyle and sexuality whilst silently assassinating their character and dress sense.

I watched an obviously drunken couple arguing outside on the pavement. I looked on at the ensuing argument with a mixture of amazement and bemused wonder, but it was passing the time and keeping me amused. I took a sip of coffee and lit a cigarette as I contemplated possible gift ideas and pondered the best way to forever capture the radiant Nikki's heart, as I felt sure that she was heaven-sent.

Eventually with coffee drained, cigarette smoked and my appetite (at least for the moment) sated, I decided to leave the sanctuary of the café and peruse the market in the hope of finding a suitable gift for Nikki.

As I stepped outside the strains of Bob Marley reverberated from a passing car that was as old as Methuselah and seemingly with only the rust holding it together. A car alarm was going off somewhere in the distance and a Staffordshire bull terrier barked aggressively from behind a chain-link fence.

Welcome to the city that was supposedly paved with gold, a land of milk and honey. Welcome to paradise...

The tips of the leaves were yellowing on the trees whilst the dazzle of the sun was lighting up the grey clouds in the sky. The air was still balmy, despite the breeze of the traffic. There was a ridiculously large amount of cars about considering the condition of the roads here and the size of the crowds, so I felt a shortness of breath and nasal irritation as I was left with little choice but to inhale their noxious exhaust fumes.

A few doors away from the cafeteria I discovered a tattoo parlour. I paused momentarily in the midst of the crowd as I caught a glimpse of my long autumnal hair reflected in the shop window and noted that with the light from the sun it blazed like an auburn halo. From force of habit I glanced at the tattoos on the display chart there but I fought the urge to go in, as I decided a long time ago that three were more than enough.

Several biker types stood outside the shop, glaring at me, their frown lines deepening with every passing second. Obviously I met with their disapproval but refusing to be intimidated I returned their gaze with equal distaste. They looked as though they were no strangers to prison and far from a great advertisement for the tattooist inside the parlour I would have thought. Although, in this day and age, maybe not?

God, sometimes I felt my rapidly advancing years...

Continuing along the pavement, I passed stalls set out with make up, clothes, compact discs, books and a variety of bric-a-brac. I wanted to avoid Ladbroke Grove, which was the skid row part of town if I could, as that had been in the in the clutches of decay and crime for a good few years now. I so hoped that I found a suitable gift soon as I did not really wish to abort the search.

I thought that it would be such a nice touch to arrive on Nikki's doorstep, bearing gifts. I wished now that I had remembered to check which perfume she wore. Fortunately for me, minutes later I had found a stall selling a variety of alternative, pagan and gothic style jewellery. As I stepped closer and looked over the top of the display cabinets a beautiful silver bracelet with a large rainbow moonstone inset caught my eye. I studied it dreamily, as it was beautiful, feminine and delicate and totally encapsulated everything that Nikki epitomised. I had always believed that jewellery was a proper token of affection, and this was a beautiful piece, so was too elated to even bother haggling over the asking price.

I dipped into my trouser pocket and handed over the money to the stallholder, who was a young girl with light strawberry blonde braided hair, blue eyes and pretty skin. Her short tatty stone-washed denim skirt (that looked at least a size too small for her) and her long 'Nu Rock' boots unfortunately did her no favours, but I assumed that it was what all the teenagers were now wearing (they tended to be so dictated by fashion and having the right label that they would wear a potato sack if you stuck a FCUK label on it).

With no preamble the stallholder placed the bracelet into a gorgeous black display box that had a delightful blood-red satin lining, and which set the jewellery off perfectly. She then placed the box into a small plastic bag, embossed with the company logo, and handed the item over to me. She smiled and mouthed a thank you, which I found myself reciprocating. I glanced at my watch but could not remember what time Nikki had said that she generally arrived back home from the salon. Perhaps I would take a nice leisurely stroll back to my apartment via her house, just on the off chance that she was already in. If not I would telephone her later as I had originally planned. The last twenty-four hours had been a complete success and I felt totally gratified. A memory of our lovemaking flashed behind my eyes as a tiny smile tweaked my lips. I was counting the minutes until I could feast my gaze upon Nikki again as my body was full of eagerness and I loathed having time to kill…

CHAPTER 4

TARGET

It was 9:05 pm before Nikki arrived back at her house and she would be grateful to get inside out of the chilled night air, as for the last few hours she had been just another frustrated traveller monitoring the numerous tube delays and cancellations. She had been on her feet all day and now most of the evening and so she was looking forward to pampering herself with a long soak in a hot bubble bath, surrounded by aromatic candles and a chilled glass or two of Nicolas Feuillatte Brut Champagne. In her mind, there was nothing more relaxing than steeping in a foam bath infused with the pure essential oils of sandalwood, rose and cedar, and topping up the hot water at regular intervals. It was continuous hedonistic pleasure, innocently luxurious and self-indulgent, but she felt as though she had deserved it.

She mused that it had been a relatively good day thus far, transport problems aside, as she had made love to a really sweet guy in the morning, spent the day with a shop full of satisfied clients and the takings were up again for the third week running.

She reached down into her handbag for her purse and as usual fumbled inside it for her front door key. Once found, she removed it and slid the key into the lock. Just as she was turning it and the door was opening she felt a gloved hand move quickly across her mouth, stifling her intended scream. She saw the glint of steel as a knife was waved in front of her face then placed at her throat. Sheer panic and terror engulfed her instantly. She felt her bladder involuntarily empty itself as a result of the fear and the sense of complete helplessness that she felt. She sensed that she was about to die. She did not try to turn around but her mind was desperately trying to conjure up an escape plan. She tasted the beaten leather of her assailant's gloved hand as it grasped her mouth, stifling any of her potential cries for help. She was shoved through the front door, her black stiletto ankle boots buckling under her, so she ended up falling face down on to the hall carpet, as she heard the sound of the front door being decisively shut behind her.

Survival instinct came rushing to the fore as she kicked out and began clawing viciously at her attacker whilst trying to scramble to a location of safety but it was all too late and in vain as she felt gloved hands now clasp tightly around her exposed neck.

She gasped for air, her face reddening as she clawed at her own neck in a vain bid to release the assailant's hands. She was aching and breathless and could feel the life ever inching from her. She tried to conjure a scream, a final fight for life but could find no voice. She was physically overwhelmed and could no longer feel air, her breath weak and rasping, as her strength ebbed away. She smelled pungently of urine and fear as her life flashed before her eyes and the only sound she could hear was her own rasping respirations, before the silence and the darkness were complete.

As her body flopped lifelessly on to the carpet her assailant knew that she had died prettily. He knelt down, squatting beside her (pondering the way that her face had retained its beauty, even in death) before planting a gentle kiss on her cheek. He was pleased to note that his hunger had not stolen the innocence from her eyes. He arose and stalked into the living room, before peering out of its window. He was delighted to note that everything was still and that there was no sound or movement on the pavement or road outside. That was good as he did not wish to be disturbed. He felt wickedly pleased as he contemplated switching on the light, but he dared not risk it just yet. After a moment of thought he reached out and drew the curtains tight.

His hand had already snaked into his trousers long before he had turned and walked back across the room to his victim.

CHAPTER 5

CRIME SCENE

The property was cordoned off by the crime scene ribbon that fluttered in the breeze as a barrier of uniformed police officers protected the scene from the assorted passing rubbernecks. Obviously there was nothing too riveting on the television tonight.

Detective Inspector Ross, who had just arrived at the house, absently flashed his warrant card at the guarding officers before flicking his gaze down and ducking underneath the police tape to enter the premises. He was less than amused to get a call like this on what, until then, had been his only day off for almost a fortnight.

His tight skin allowed little expression as he sucked in his breath and his eyes flickered reluctantly across the scene, studying it with detachment. He had witnessed too many such scenes in his long career to become too emotional. His face stayed impassive, although opposite him in the doorway, clearly outlined, he had now spotted the body of the young dead woman. With the soiling and her disturbed clothing the slumped corpse resembled a sleeping drunk but he knew instantly from the marks around her neck, that this murder was exactly like the previous three that he had recently attended. His jaw tightened at the recollection. All the women had been strangled as they entered their homes approaching nightfall.

Two young uniformed police officers were standing with Detective Sergeant Armstrong and Detective Constable Regan to the rear of the hallway, notebooks in hand as scene of crime officers, attired in white plastic suits, crouched down on their hands and knees, vacuuming trace evidence and bagging and tagging what they hoped would be relevant fibres and samples to lead to a successful conviction. Fingerprint powder covered the front door, walls and door frames, whilst strips of clear tape were placed upon glass slides and tucked away inside a currently half open metal briefcase that housed their crime scene kits. The pathologist, whose face was pale and grim, leaned against the back wall whilst orating his findings into a Dictaphone, which he gripped like a much treasured possession.

Detective Inspector Ross's impatience came to the fore as he desperately longed to get stuck in. He was itching to commence his part in the proceedings, but his hands were tied until the scene of crime officers and the pathologist had finished their preliminaries and the crime scene photographs were taken.

His brow was furrowed in thought, whilst his mind and body itched to get started and to begin the process that he hoped would bring the serial killer, of yet another relatively young woman, to trial.

As anger boiled within him, he approached Detective Sergeant Armstrong and Detective Constable Regan and the two uniformed officers that they were conversing with. He would demand a full accounting as he needed to get himself updated as to any possible witnesses and to verify exactly who had phoned in the 999 emergency calls. He needed to get the house-to- house inquiries going as soon as possible, whilst the killers trail was still relatively warm. Surely someone must have seen something out of the ordinary, especially if the killer had the house under surveillance for some time?

He felt that he was long overdue a break in these murder cases as currently the press and media were having an absolute field day at his expense. He knew though that he had been in the force long enough to not be surprised by their diatribe. He let out a long sigh of exasperation, standing there waiting was getting on his nerves as he had so many lines of enquiry to pursue and someone must have something worth telling. He reached into his jacket pocket to remove his notebook and pen as feelings of déjà-vu surfaced within him. With a shiver he recognised the depressing truth that this would soon happen again if an arrest did not follow swiftly. He knew that it was his job to prevent crime and he himself had a wife, a mother and two daughters all within the London area and he felt that he was currently failing in his duty to protect them (as well as society).

Unwilling to accept failure so easily, he recognised that his options were fast disappearing and that it was time to throw the dice and gamble. There would be no more deaths now as he was determined to take control.

CHAPTER 6

ROUTINE

I felt exhausted but I knew sleep was near impossible as insomnia had been my partner for more years than I cared to remember. An unenviable consequence of my fractious relationships and severely dysfunctional childhood.

Solitude fell across my heart like a hazy reflection as I took a long drag on my cigarette, before flicking the butt out of the partially opened window.

Reclining on my well upholstered leather recliner I cleared my throat and reached for the phone to redial the telephone number from the Post-it note that Nikki had handed me, in her home, before we parted. With each unanswered ring, I felt a stab of disappointment. Again it rang ten times before cutting on to the now sadly all too familiar voice message: "Hi, it's Nikki, I am unable to come to the phone right now, so please leave your name, telephone number and a brief message and I will call you back as soon as I am available."

I waited for the tone... "Hi, it's Jamie, I hope everything is OK. I would love to see you again, so please call me when you get an opportunity. My mobile number is: 07930 117570".

That was the message I had left last night and now again this morning. I wondered why she had not returned my call and was not picking up the telephone or any of her messages. I was sure that she had liked me... hadn't she?

Yes, of course she did, she would not have given me her correct telephone number otherwise would she, I surmised as I desperately tried to reassure myself.

I longed to speak with her in person and relive every moment of yesterday's delicious erotic drama as she truly made my heart race. I ached to hear more of her entertaining stories and to be able to hold and caress her, whilst running my hands through her long flaxen hair. Perhaps I should go over there as even if she is not in I could always pop a card through the door along with the bracelet (which still boxed, currently sat upon my coffee table, like a discarded Christmas present).

I had been awake all night as I was longing for Nikki to telephone me and I did not want to miss her call through being asleep.

I sighed and picked up my mug of coffee. It was cold and had already skinned over, but I drank it down anyway.

I felt aimless and bored. I started replaying the conversations Nikki and I had in my mind, as if I had not run through them enough during the early hours of this morning when sleep had once again so cruelly eluded me. I could hear her voice, picture her face and even smell her perfume (I really must remember to find out which brand it was).

The memory of the attraction I had felt for her was just all too great. The ending of my marriage had dealt my self-esteem an all too serious blow. One, at the time, I felt was critical. Still my confidence needed emotional reassurance and I knew that I could not bear never to see Nikki again. I closed my eyes and let the feelings flow as I had been told that letting my feelings out was the first step to my recovery, instead of bottling them up as I had been doing for more years than I now cared to remember.

Suddenly startled my self- analysis and contemplation came to an abrupt conclusion as my mobile phone rang. With the speed of a striking cobra I quickly snatched up the phone.

"Hello", I cried expectantly, relief coursing through my veins, as I assumed (wrongly) that it was Nikki on the other end of the line. I was to be sorely disappointed as a man's gruff voice introduced himself as Detective Sergeant Armstrong.

My grip tightened on the phone as I was briefly taken aback. I swore silently under my breath, before I managed to stammer a reply. The words had jammed in my throat as my mind was whirling. I was informed that there had been an incident involving a Miss Nikki Chandler and the officer at the other end of the line enquired as to how well I knew her. I felt instantly uneasy and I could sense my forehead creasing into a puzzled frown.

I stammered uncontrollably as I tried to explain that I had only known Nikki for less than forty-eight hours. A sudden surge of panic made my head hurt and a wave of doubt flooded my eyes.

I dipped towards disbelief but fought my way back as Detective Sergeant Armstrong took my full name and address (as he apparently only had my mobile number which he had obtained from Nikki's answering machine) and said he would be over in an hour or so, whereupon he would explain everything to me in more detail. My words had come out sounding empty, the elation that had surged only moments before was drained by the sudden turn of events. I yearned to ask more but the officer's tone and impatient snap signalled that I should end the discussion, seemingly refusing to discuss the matter further.

My composure had now cracked completely so I could no longer relax and felt severe discomfort as I had an odd uncomfortable feeling, like icy fingers running over my flesh. My stomach was fluttering as I knew something was wrong. Had Nikki been in an accident? Was she under arrest? Why was he being so cagey and why would he not tell me anything?!

I was fired with curiosity but just could not shake off the slightly dispirited and disconcerted feeling that Detective Sergeant Armstrong had given me. I drew in a long shuddering breath as I felt a sudden stab of unease. Just why was I feeling under so much pressure?

I closed my eyes for a brief moment whilst trying to make sense of the call and dreading that something bad had happened to Nikki. A dozen different hypotheses flashed through my mind, each one more obscure and distressing than the last. A cold sick dread coiled in my stomach and squeezed. I tried to fight against it but seemed unable to overcome the anxiety completely.

God, I needed a drink.

Needing to regain my poise, I arose from the arm chair and headed towards the liquor cabinet which sat in the corner of the room (as if an enticing flame to a moth). I unstopped the brandy decanter before pouring myself a more than healthy shot. Raising the tumbler to my lips I took a generous gulp and immediately felt the burning sensation ignite my throat and chest. I knew that I was on the brink of a slippery slope, unable to resist the hard liquor and now yielding to it. I sensed that this would be the first of a great many today, as I had been drinking a lot of late, never able to totally abstain, the temptation all too great. I felt shame that drink had become such an integral part of my lifestyle.

Hours later my train of thought, that had until this point been spiralling hopelessly out of control, was lost as the doorbell rang. My head was still spinning as I tentatively approached the front door and upon opening it I was confronted by two tall thickset men, both with short dark receding hair that was slightly greying at the temples. Their stances were ramrod straight as warrant cards were flashed in front of my face, but I did not really need to study them as I could tell a copper a mile off, plain clothes or not. I think it was something to do with the intoxication of power and the god complex they all appeared to adopt. Struggling against instinct, I stepped aside to let them enter the apartment and closed the door behind them as I ushered them into the living room.

"I am Detective Sergeant Armstrong, we spoke on the phone, and my colleague here is Detective Constable Regan. I am sorry to call on you like this but we do need to ask you a few questions about your relationship with Miss Chandler."

(I could not help but note that the last time I had seen faces like theirs I was feeding them bananas).

As the officer spoke he fixed me with his deep set eyes that I noted were cold and unfriendly, and I sensed that he had taken an instant dislike to me, as I had him. His eyes were as flat and emotionless as his voice and I was now wishing that I'd had a good night's sleep as I was becoming concerned that this was something beyond a routine enquiry and something far more serious. I could feel deep furrows forming on my previously smooth brow whilst my pulse had begun pounding like a fist upon a door. My wandering thoughts were interrupted as Detective Sergeant Armstrong explained that a woman they believed to be a Miss Nikki Chandler had been found strangled in the early hours of this morning and as a murder enquiry had now been launched, they were naturally keen to speak to relatives, friends, neighbours, and basically anyone else who had known her.

I was in shock, my mind reeling, as I desperately tried to blank out the news that I was now receiving. I felt a silent cry of outrage and grief well within me, and I felt so empty that I ached. With the news of Nikki the loneliness which I hoped would be assuaged forever, had come back and, it seemed, more painfully and urgently than ever. It just could not be true, my mind, at first, refusing to accept it as I gripped the chair, in which I was seated, for support. My expression was frozen as my mind cried out in unbearable anguish. I just wanted to scream and rage at the blind injustice of it all but no sound would come. I had only just started to believe that some stability in my life was possible and now this happens...

I felt numb as my stomach clenched and I winced at the realization that my life had been robbed of all meaning. My mind screamed for the foil strip of Prozac that sat in the bathroom cabinet, as every sense of my previous foreboding had now became an all too crushing reality. I was too tired to cope as after just one day of heaven my pain, despair and emotional instability were now as raw and intense as ever. My eyes prickled as the light trembled within them and I felt the seeds of a tension headache coming on as the pain snarling a warning shot between my eyes.

Detective Sergeant Armstrong stifled a sigh and continued glancing at his notes before once again maintaining eye contact with me, demanding my attention. He stared at me, frowning as if he were perplexed by the welcome they had received. The truth was that both the officers made me feel intensely uncomfortable and I was inexplicably wary of them. For some reason I felt as if I were a rodent frozen under a cobra's gaze, the apprehension trembling in my eyes.

I could feel the trickle of sweat along the back of my neck and the perspiration on my brow. I was totally unable to grasp, and in truth, not wanting to believe the things that I was now being told as they seemed inexplicable. I could hear the shock in my tone and was beginning to feel very panicky and claustrophobic, although I knew that I had done nothing wrong. I took a deep breath and my shoulders slumped as I leaned forward to grasp the edge of the table for support, my body having turned to jelly, sick with a mixture of, anxiety and foreboding. I felt my lips pinch shut and my expression must have looked puzzled as I lapsed into silence, my mind trying unsuccessfully to make sense of the bizarre.

I only wished that I could have hidden my head in the sand, like an ostrich, as at present I still felt like I just wanted to scream and protest loudly and bitterly at the blind injustice of it all. I felt full of grief, outrage and disbelief, a broken connection like a scattered rainbow.

I sensed that my only chance of happiness had now been snatched away forever and I felt like a silent portrait of misery.

A sense of shame and awkwardness fell upon me but both police officers were scowling and looked suitably unimpressed.

I could feel Detective Sergeant Armstrong's hackles rising as he felt that I was being deliberately obstructive. He eyed me with poorly veiled suspicion, his brow was furrowed and his forehead almost creased into simian-type wrinkles. The flat look in his eyes revealed that he just did not understand that I was plainly unable to give him many of the answers that he vainly searched for. The officers spoke impatiently and often repeated their questions, whilst totally negating the fact that at that precise moment I was having a panic attack or to even spot that my fists were clenched so tightly, with my nails digging deep into the palms of my hands, that they were forming welts. When I did speak I could hear the trembling in my voice and I could tell that neither of the two detectives seated in front of me, believed a single word that I was saying and the instant dislike they had taken to me was now fully vindicated in their minds. I felt blinkered by grief or perhaps I was just using it to flee my own painful memories...

Due to my many run-ins with the local constabulary as a juvenile I had never since trusted the police and these two officers had the bedside manner of Dr Crippen, so I was left feeling distinctly less than assured by their intimidating presence. They seemed to be eyeing me reproachfully, their expressions baleful. I could now feel my emotions charging the room, so felt that the officers had long since outstayed their welcome.

I attempted to hem in my thoughts as I could not have cared less how they might feel about me. They could dissect my behaviour if they wished as it would be no skin off my nose, and if they wanted to throw their weight around to feel like men and to compensate for their inadequacy between the sheets, then the problem was theirs, not mine (how I pitied their partners and the officer's ignorant little minds). I was not usually that bitchy but the unfurling events were fast testing my temper and patience.

Unaware of my inward thoughts, I could feel their gaze upon me but I did not bother to raise my eyes to meet their stares as I was too busy trying to gather my own thoughts. My face was tight with anger and indignation and I ensured that my responses, when they came, were curt and clipped as I hissed back. Smouldering rage had now driven out my earlier growing unease but I still felt as if I had lost my soul.

The officers were both as bright as an eclipse and were becoming an annoyance, if not a problem, as I just wished to be left alone to grieve and to try and gather my currently confused and terrifying thoughts.

Just why the hell did they fail to understand this?

Luckily the confrontation ended soon after, whereupon both police officers stood up and with an icy glance thanked me for my time. They informed me that obviously the investigations would be continuing and that they may need to speak to me again at a later date.

I took a deep shaky breath before mumbling something noncommittal back, whilst thinking that I could easily wait.

Their response was to fix me with an expressionless stare, but thankfully no further words were exchanged.

My anger burned bright and hot as I closed the door behind them, and all the memories of my past humiliation, my hurt, pain and embarrassments came flooding back to me. The indignity and irrationality of the circumstances appalled me, so becoming increasingly upset I sank to my knees and wept. Tears were suddenly flowing down my cheeks as I felt that my world was caving in on me. Once again I felt so alone, so afraid and vulnerable as my life appeared to lurch from one crisis to another.

The gods had obviously forsaken me.

Heartbroken, I fell to my knees, chest heaving, struggling for breath. For several seconds I just crouched there, unable to move.

My chest tightened again as tears formed a lump in my throat and my stomach clenched. I had lost all control as I began to shake. With my heart broken, my mind sprang open the stoppered well of grief before I could cork it shut. I was once again that twelve year old boy thrust into the lion's den with no one there to help me...

Almost an hour later, I sat inert, hunched over a lukewarm cup of coffee and a discarded plate of cold toast as tears continued to cascade down my face. I could not believe my luck in finding someone as perfect as Nikki but how much I was now grieving for Nikki and how much was self pity for my blighted life was still open to debate. I felt a pang of conscience and despised myself for my selfishness, but too much had happened in too short a space of time for me to really comprehend it all (or to be certain how much of it had actually happened at all). Life just seemed so meaningless and no longer worth my trouble, and that scared me. I sensed that the answers were naggingly present but as ever out of reach to me.

They do say you can't see the wood for the trees.

My body shuddered and convulsed, whilst my mind remained numb and frozen from the shock. Inside me the pain and anguish I felt seemed to resonate from every cell. My tears blinded me as inside I went numb, whilst my mind felt dark and dead as the pain began to fester within me. I sat in my chair, half asleep as delving into my inner self had left me feeling exhausted...

'Nikki', I said... I was retreating back into my own little world. A half smile flitted across my lips as I could hear the sound of Nikki's voice inside my head. The pain stopped briefly and happiness fleetingly returned until I realised that I was just daydreaming. As I reluctantly prised my eyes open she was gone, whereupon the sadness, tiredness and hollowness returned with a vengeance. I felt like I was going to pass out so I walked to the liquor cabinet and fixed myself a stiff drink as once again my mind drifted painfully...

The hands of my mind tried to grab Nikki back but my previous day's happiness was now just a dim and distant memory (as if just a dream that had now become a crushing nightmare full of pain and emptiness and sorrow). I struggled to focus as a feeling of unreality fell upon me like a cloak and painful thoughts ripped at my mind...

My soul was now a chasm of darkness and all that I wanted to do was fulminate as Nikki had made me feel special and somehow responsible for her. Had there been any way that I could have saved her? Guilt was now gathering solidly inside me, leaving me anxious and misunderstood. I felt acutely lonely, just why were things never straightforward and simple?

Just why would someone murder such a sweet and innocent person? The question so unfathomable that it could have no answer. I felt deep resentment and a desire for vindictive revenge, I wanted to tear the killer apart with my bare hands, yet I was so helpless and totally powerless. Nikki was just so full of life; she did not deserve to be a victim.

I would not have minded throwing in my hand.

Given the choice, I would have taken her place willingly.

CHAPTER 7

THE ONGOING INVESTIGATION

The CID team, led by Detective Inspector Ross, were situated in the incident room where they were desperately scrutinizing the white board, which was covered with photographs and notes on all of the four known female victims to date, desperately seeking the connection that would lead them to the perpetrator.

On the surface there did not appear to be a common link as the women were all of different age ranges, social status and hair types. There had to be something deeper...perhaps a personality trait that the killer had spotted? Unless of course they were just entirely random and just happened to be in the wrong place at the wrong time? They let the unanswered question float in the air.

Well-thumbed photocopies of the crime analysis report forms sat on the table in front of them, surrounded by overflowing ashtrays and plastic cups with varying amounts of beverages within them.

Detective Inspector Ross, who had called the meeting stood in front of his team. He was an intimidating figure of a man who possessed the assurance that came with power and possessed a strong sense of self. He stood six foot two inches tall and had a broad shouldered thick set build, which was currently confined in a white shirt (with the sleeves rolled up to his elbows) and smart navy blue pleated trousers. A shock of steel grey hair and piercing, almost wolverine, grey eyes only added to his no nonsense demeanour.

Detective Inspector Ross cleared his throat and addressed his assembled team. His voice boomed out across the floor.

"Morning, gentlemen, as you know we have four unsolved murders on our hands and both the local and national media are having an absolute field day at our expense. We now have full identification and forensics on the first three victims and we should be getting the analysis on the fourth within a day or so."

As he spoke he realised that this was turning into the toughest test of his career to date. He knew that his future promotion ambitions rested on a quick result and conviction. Fail and he would remain at his present rank until retirement. As he spoke his chin jerked up and eyes blazed.

"I know most of you have been up all night but we must strike while the iron is hot. We need every bit of evidence we can get our hands on. I want detailed house-to-house enquiries, I want Miss Chandler's house torn apart, interview her neighbours, her friends and work colleagues. Ask them if they saw anyone loitering around her home or business premises. I want to know about lovers, boyfriends etc, as this bastard must be getting close to his victims somehow. Leave no stone unturned. Let me know about anyone who sets alarm bells ringing, as I want this scumbag nailed as soon as possible. Oh, and one of you get round to the morgue and ring me as soon as her parents have given their formal identification of the body."

The team disbanded to their duties and Detective Inspector Ross was left alone to retreat behind his desk. He shot up his sleeve and checked his watch before he reached down and grabbed his cigarette packet and lighter off the desk. He lit his last cigarette, tossing the now empty packet towards the bin. It missed. He poured more coffee into the polystyrene cup that was placed upon his desk and then proceeded to painstakingly go through the compilation of data, photographs, witness statements, pathology and forensic reports that were currently piled up in front of him, convinced that somewhere buried within them was the crucial information that held the key to solving these crimes, a common denominator that just could not be ignored. He knew that if he failed to crack these cases his already well-established fast-track promotion ladder was likely to be pulled out from under him... forever. His every waking hour was devoted to furthering his position within the force. He could never admit defeat and suffer losing face. He knew that must not be allowed to happen as in his relentless pursuit of position self-preservation was everything.

CHAPTER 8

FROM DESPAIR TO WHERE?

I found sleep elusive despite my raging fatigue as my mind had been working overtime fending off my demons whilst continuing to scatter my thoughts in all directions. I could not even remember the last time that I'd had a straight night's sleep as I had been unable to stop the questions and bad dreams pounding away like a jackhammer in my mind. Even when I reached brief moments of unconsciousness, bad dreams and terrible images soon shot me back to reality. With the anxiety and misery I felt lonelier now than before Nikki had come into my life. Nothing in my life seemed to make sense anymore, the unfairness of which almost took my breath way.

My face felt drawn and my eyes itchy and bloodshot as I lay on the couch, my exhaustion too great. My hands were tucked behind my head as I stared up, counting the cracks in the ceiling.

(Twelve…I really must get it re-plastered).

The sun had barely filtered through the now permanently drawn curtains. I had been smoking like the proverbial chimney, as my appetite had deserted me days ago, hence the apartment reeked of stale cigarette smoke, whilst half drunk cups of coffee, most filled with discarded cigarette butts, littered every available flat surface. The kitchen sink was piled sky high with dirty crockery, cutlery and a variety of saucepans, as I had not washed up for many days.

I could feel the stubble itching on my chin but for the moment I could not find the energy to get up and shave. A gloom, that I had failed to shake off settled over me as I reflected. I found that my spirit had been crushed, my soul destroyed and suicide played on my mind as I had no one to comfort me, to help me ease the searing pain that I now felt deep inside. I felt distinctly uneasy, the hurt and anguish striking me like an arrow as tears ambushed me again. I grieved for myself as much as for the loss of Nikki. I felt a little stirring of guilt at this realization as I felt somehow responsible for her death although I was not quite sure why.

The thought struck me that no one would shed a tear for my demise when it eventually came. That hopefully, would be sooner rather than later. I knew that there could never be anyone else that I could love. It was as if Nikki had made a cage for me and once I entered the key had been thrown away, so no-one else could ever penetrate my space.

With a sigh, I rose sluggishly up from the settee, shook my stiff legs to aid the circulation and trudged reluctantly off to the bathroom to empty my aching bladder, which was currently demanding immediate relief. I snapped on the light, wincing at the bulb's brightness, and then once my eyes had re-adjusted, I studied my visage in the mirror. I felt a ripple of shock and felt as though I might vomit. God, I looked awful...my skin was pale and clammy, hair matted and tousled; face crumpled and unshaven and I had bags under my eyes the size of suitcases. Thinking that I should at least make some sort of effort at grooming I ran a brush through my hair and then reached into the glass bathroom cabinet for the electric razor, not trusting myself with a cut throat one in my present frame of mind (although I was not afraid of death as, from my earliest memory, life to me had always been a very painful experience).

I closed my eyes for a brief moment and took a deep breath before I continued; trying to close off my emotions and shut myself off from the self-destructive thoughts that currently bombarded my brain. I felt like I wanted to tear the world apart as I was being driven in a direction that I did not want to go. The realization struck me that I did not even know when Nikki's funeral was and I felt certain that the police would be less than forthcoming regarding the funeral date or any of the arrangements.

I had to face the truth; the reality was that I knew so little about Nikki, in life and now in death.

That fleeting moment of happiness and contentment, when our lives entwined, was now lost forever.

My demons which were once driven underground were now back with a vengeance and my already low self-esteem had reached rock bottom. I was devastated and was too confused to think clearly about anything at the moment.

Just why was I destined to never have a meaningful sexual relationship? Why was I so pathetic and worthless? The questions struck like daggers, tearing into my soul. I felt sure that I could never love or be loved again. I could not help but think that life would just be so simple if only we could keep all the good memories and erase the bad, as at present it seemed, if you were lucky, that the memories may fade with time, but the deep scars lingered for all of eternity.

Perhaps I was just being too bitter and cynical?

As my frustration spilled out in a long sigh my mind was desperately searching for a reason to keep going...

After relieving my aching bladder I made for the shower, hoping that the warm jets of water would ease my tense and aching muscles and help to relax my tortured and tormented mind. After a few minutes under the shower I felt the tension slightly easing as the water jets gently massaged my taut skin. I felt slightly more revived and definitely more human.

I closed my eyes, as the realization that I had no-one in my life, stung me again. I knew that I was not alone through choice as from as early as I could remember all that I had ever wanted was to be loved. How I longed for someone to be there for me, to hug and hold me, to comfort me and to stop the hurting. Just to tell me that everything would be alright and to dissipate this helpless frustration that I felt had severely blighted my life.

Ablutions over, I switched off the water control and stepped out of the shower, wrapping towels around my hair and torso as I made my way to the kitchen. I walked past the shelves full of exotic herbs and spices that lined the kitchen walls to the sink where I turned on the kitchen tap to fill the kettle. The cold jet of water accidentally splashed my previously warm chest, so sending a shiver through me as I recoiled.

I put a spoonful of coffee and two of sugar into the mug and waited for the kettle to boil. Unfortunately I had nothing-stronger left to drink in the apartment so I had to settle for simple comforts. The empty Remy Martin Cognac bottles seemed to be smirking at me from the bin like a guilty secret.

I was not sure what was causing my urge to drink excessively of late as I'd not had a drinking problem prior to this year.

Fortunately the coffee was strong and the caffeine kicked in immediately.

I was so lost in my thoughts that I barely registered the doorbell's first ring. When it rang for a second time I distractedly wandered to the door. I wished, at times like this, that I'd had an entry phone or peephole installed, as I was in no mood for visitors. If it was bleeding Jehovah's Witnesses, I would tell them exactly where they could stick their bloody watchtower literature!

With reluctance I opened the door and to my shock I was confronted by Detective Sergeant Armstrong and Detective Constable Regan (the gruesome twosome). With hindsight I would now have preferred the Jehovah's Witnesses. I must have looked shocked as the Detectives explained they had been trying to reach me on my mobile phone but kept getting my voicemail messaging service and to which I had failed to respond to any of the messages they had previously left.

(Tut Tut)

I apologised, explaining that I had switched my mobile off a few days ago and had obviously forgotten to turn it back on.

It was just a little white lie. The truth was that I was in no mood for callers, of any kind.

I reluctantly stepped aside and flourishing an unlit cigarette beckoned them to enter.

"I have just put the kettle on if you fancy a brew?"

I was desperately trying to play the gracious host, although in truth if I never saw them again it would not be a moment too soon. I had never liked or respected the police so I understandably felt edgy and tense having them back here, sitting in my home, invading my space and privacy. The offer of refreshment was abruptly declined... I should have known that my anxiety to show hospitality to the police would merely be seen as an ingratiating tactic, showing a yearning to cover something up. I despaired.

Turning away from them, I went over to the curtains and pulled them open, then undid the window latch to allow some much needed air and ventilation into the room, as the apartment currently resembled and smelled like a seedy poker den. I looked up at my artwork that adorned the walls, dark themed paintings that tended toward the macabre. I found them an outlet for my pain...sombre pictures that reflected my un-illuminated life.

I sighed and headed back into the kitchen, whilst scanning the raised surfaces for my lighter.

The atmosphere noticeably darkened around the kitchen table as I returned to it. The three of us sat staring at each other but initially saying nothing. It reminded me of one of those tense saloon scenes in spaghetti westerns, moments before the big gunfight...that the one with the white hat invariably won.

An oppressive atmosphere hung in the air, which you could have cut with a knife.

"Have there been any developments?" I asked cautiously.

"Well, we would like you to accompany us to the police station, if you could, to answer a few further questions and to hopefully assist us with our ongoing enquiries."

Their eyes were flat and hard and unyielding, their expressions blank.

"Can I not just answer them here?" I retorted, not really fancying the prospect of spending half the day cooped up inside a police interview room.

My mind had already tumbled into dark places and grief shuddered through me as I spoke.

"If you are refusing to come with us, we would have no option but to arrest you," replied Detective Sergeant Armstrong, matter of factly.

I almost fainted in shock, but instead started shaking violently, no doubt my face ashen as my body started to perspire. My chest tightened again and tears formed a lump in my throat and welled in my eyes. I felt pain and anger in somewhat equal dosage.

"What?!" I cried. "On what possible grounds?!"

"How does murder grab you?"

It was Detective Constable Regan's sardonic reply and I felt momentarily frozen as if caught in a flashbulb's glare. The fact that he was looking very pleased with himself did not make me feel any calmer.

As I was near despair, I could not keep the note of hysteria out of my voice as I responded.

"How on earth can I be a suspect?"

My question remained unanswered.

I had known Nikki less than forty-eight hours before she was cruelly stolen from me and, on my part at least, it had almost been love at first sight (and I was quite confident that she had felt the same way).

The officer's words had clung oppressively to me (like feverish heat) as I could not believe what I was now hearing. I shook my head sharply, how dare they accuse me of her murder. My previous shock had now been replaced by smouldering anger towards the two Neo Nazis that were sat opposite me. I fixed them with a look of disgust and noted that they had contempt in their eyes towards me also. Their eyes glinted coldly, like snakes, their decision made and minds obviously made up about me.

I felt slightly claustrophobic in their intimidating presence, the tension growing every second as my mind flitted back to childhood memories and 'the gang'. Grief shuddered through me as my breath shook and rage thundered in my temples as I felt myself becoming angry with them again.

Lack of sleep and no doubt my medication were only adding to my increasing sense of paranoia. I shook my head in a gesture of what I hoped would be taken as exasperation and righteous indignation, but the officers pretended not to notice. I felt helplessly frustrated as people were so ignorant. They have never understood me. I was always the one they laughed at, threatened by my intelligence. Well I was sick of being their caged animal, I was no longer that twelve-year-old boy and I did not appreciate being mocked by two fascist pigs, which were driving me to distraction. I felt that they were trying to intimidate me and undermine me, to get under my skin. I had the vague sensation of being caught in a spider's web but I chuckled inwardly as I'd had to handle men like these since the tender age of twelve. This was nothing new, like water off a duck's back …or so I tried to kid myself.

"I need to put some clothes on."

"Fine."

As I hurled away my still unlit cigarette, the officers gazed blindly at me, their eyes never moving. As they remained seated

I got up and walked to the bedroom to get dressed. As I was changing I glanced out of the window, noting the overcast sky and the rain soaked shrubbery. The gloomy weather appeared to be mirroring my emotions and the events that were now taking place around me. The more I thought about it, the more I fumed. I felt more annoyed than worried now, so I took a deep breath as I tried to maintain my self-control. I had been bullied and beaten since as early as I could remember and had learned the harsh lessons of self-control the hard way. The rule was never to let them see that you are hurting and never let them know when they have found your Achilles heel as it only encourages them and reveals your weak points for future spite. Unfortunately the feat in my present frame of mind was easier said than done. I had to give the officers no sign of wearing me down (though I now regretted surrendering to their demands). I closed my eyes and took a deep breath to collect myself, and then stifling a sharp pang of grief I pushed myself from the bedroom. I fully understood their machinations and the purport of their discussions, so with thinly disguised contempt I returned dressed to the two detectives and with an expressionless stare, said coolly, "Right, shall we go then?"

The officers, who were not trying too hard to cover their self-satisfied smirks, did not raise any objection…

CHAPTER 9

INTERROGATION

As I leant back in the chair I could feel my stomach churning, whilst the tensions inside me felt like an icy hand squeezing within my chest. I gritted my teeth so hard that they hurt but I carefully tried to keep my face without expression as I did not want the officers to read my thoughts, although inside my anxiety was growing with every passing second. I knew that sleep and I were once again to be strangers tonight. I closed my eyes as the heady cocktail of agony and fury washed over me. I could not understand the officers' knee-jerk reaction and was certain that I had better things to do than while away the hours in a (unfortunately) not too unfamiliar police interview room.

Footsteps echoed down a distant corridor and I felt a chill run across my shoulders and down my back as I listened. I had been inside many police stations in my time and suffered many beatings at the hands of officers during my teenage years (as a rent boy with a quick wit and a smart mouth tended not to be the flavour of the month with the homophobic local constabularies).

In my mind a grainy image sparkled to life...

God bless the Metropolitan Police, you had to love them...

A trickle of cold sweat ran down my spine as I vainly attempted to respond in a calm, normal and concise manner to the questions that were currently bombarding my senses. I was not under arrest apparently, just 'helping the police with their enquiries'. The whole situation was absurd and the blatant awkwardness between myself and the interviewing officers was ever increasing as I hated it when people studied me and analysed me, hoping to spy the cracks that I had long since attempted to paper over. I had been trying to put the scarring of my childhood trauma and my wife's infidelity and theft behind me and to move on with my life but now this whole farce was just picking at all the old scabs. I was struggling not to argue, as I could feel the concern simmering within me. I felt very flushed and no doubt looked rather dishevelled from constantly running my hands nervously through my hair.

Detective Constable Regan slipped his hand into his jacket pocket and proceeded to produce a packet of Benson & Hedges cigarettes. Removing the cellophane he then proceeded to tap one out and hand it to me before pushing a polystyrene cup of white coffee (to which I hastily added two sugars) towards me. Obviously he was playing 'good cop' today. The interview tape was still rolling despite the temporary lull in the proceedings after Detective Sergeant Armstrong, eyes narrowing, had demanded that I answer his questions. My mind was not paying attention to any of it as I had drifted off to another realm. I liked to be alone with my thoughts and fantasies when reality bit and things conspired against me. Anyhow, most of the evening after I had left Portobello Road Market was a complete blank to me, although I did recall arriving back at my apartment and telephoning Nikki, but only getting as far as her voicemail system. Still the questions came, to which I responded as best I could, although the detectives were clearly not impressed by the answers they were now receiving. They even probed about my mental illness... how did they find out about that? Who had they been speaking to (and whatever happened to patient confidentiality)?!

I rolled my eyes; their perception of me was as flawed as hell, which was doing nothing to allay my earlier fears about them.

I felt myself frown as I scanned the room, feeling increasing anger as well as a certain resignation. My already stretched nerves ever lengthening as in my chair I squirmed with unease. Amongst the suffocating atmosphere of depression I was beginning to feel more trapped than ever before.

The officers appeared to have made little or no headway in the several hours that we had spent talking and I could sense their frustration was ever growing. Their voices were so cold I shivered in the draught, as to them the responses that I was giving were totally unsatisfactory. They informed me that they just wanted to get the facts straight. I had to raise a smile to that statement as I knew from past experience that most police officers were as straight as a corkscrew.

There was absolutely no comfort in that thought.

Their constant and repetitive questioning had threatened to start me yawning and wear down my resolve. I was asked how and where I had met Nikki, where we went, how we got there and my subsequent movements the next day.

It felt like an episode of 'This Is Your Life'.

As the police officers exchanged resigned glances I knew that they had not left their prejudices outside the interview room. At the very least they could have shown me some compassion; instead they continued to badger me. I kept being asked, over and over again, to give the details they required as to the best of my recollection. That was a joke as I had suffered temporary blackouts on and off for the last two decades as my mind appeared to shut down at stressful times. I had tried to summon some sympathy but that had fallen on deaf ears, so I was now sitting there slightly dazed and bemused as my mind churned with questions and answers, deductions and screams. I sat there frozen as my gut clenched and my mouth dried. I could only stare uncomprehendingly. I could feel their gaze upon me but I dared not meet their eyes since both officers possessed curious facial expressions, which appeared to be a mixture of tedium and seething resentment, which I thought was a look normally reserved for doctors' receptionists and trainees in hairdressing salons.

I was requested to give a DNA sample, to which I readily agreed and a swab was wiped along the inside my mouth. Eventually I was allowed to leave the police station but I had no idea as to how far the investigation had now progressed, if at all, as for the most part the detectives sat stony faced in the windowless interview room, their voices hardening with desperation as they aired their own questions, then not liking my responses, had given their own perceived version of events. Their eyes throughout the interview were cold and hard as the officers made little or no effort to hide their feelings of contempt towards me, and their lips were so taut that they were bloodless. Their sole purpose appeared to be making life unpleasant for people whose lifestyle or appearance they disapproved of, and to me their attitude did not seem very rational or particularly fair. Their expressions were ones of irritation and perplexity and being the recipient of their baleful stares meant that I felt my own anger rise within me, the atmosphere having got so intense and cloying at times that I felt physically sick by the time it was all over.

I assumed that their charm school diplomas were still in the post.

I tried to stifle my yawns as fatigue fought me for control. I'd had a hell of a day and now fury and resentment blazed through me. I desperately wanted comfort as I felt as if my life, as well as Nikki's, had been stolen forever. I'd had ripples that disturbed my life previously but this felt like a tidal wave in comparison to them. I missed Nikki so much that it burned.

I could feel my life beginning to unravel again and I could not help but remember that I had so many old scores to settle...

It was midnight before I was finally escorted towards the door and left the custody suite, turning to give the officers an indignant glare as the door closed behind me with a decisive click.

The interrogation had lasted most of the day, with the same questions being repeated over and over again. With the officers' relentless bullying and badgering I could still hear their voices echoing inside my head even now. They appeared to have taken everything wonderful that had happened between Nikki and I, and twisted it to fit within their own warped theories.

I shivered slightly as I stepped out into the bleaching light of the moon and into the cold night air, which felt distinctly cool and damp upon my skin. A steady wind blew into my face and felt like a slap. My anxiety raged and the cost of my trembling and sweating was to throw up in the gutter. I had no handkerchief, so with my sleeve I wiped away a trickle of spit that trailed from the corner of my mouth and inhaled deeply.

There were no taxi cabs in sight so despite feeling extremely weary, cold and tired I started to walk homeward through the sodium-lit streets which somehow seemed both darker and more remote than I remembered them to be.

I felt contaminated but was too fatigued to fulminate. How I yearned to be comforted and healed, to be told that everything would now be all right. To just be held and caressed would have meant so much to me at that precise moment, but I knew that I was all alone in the world and deep down accepted that I

73

probably always would be. I tried to drag my mind away from the memories but in reality I knew that there would be no escaping the ghosts of my past, which were destined to haunt my every waking moment.

I shook my head in frustration as I knew that I would never be free of my demons.

It was just something I sensed.

As I began to make my way home the heavens opened as if the gods were crying for my plight also. I could taste the rainwater as spots of rain began to prickle my face. The rain now beat down heavily, like a million tiny crystals shimmering in the reflections of the illuminated street lamps, cutting through the velvety gloom, before drumming onto the paving stones beneath my feet. I glanced into the glittering darkness ahead of me and aimed to go straight home as I was longing for the sanctuary of my apartment and the warm comfort of my bed. It had been seventy-two hours since I had last slept and my mind and body screamed desperately for respite.

CHAPTER 10

ROUTINE

A steady breeze was keeping the pollution from hazing the pale blue sky and the sun was streaming through the open windows as I glanced at my watch for the umpteenth time. I had awoken again at first light. What I would not have given for an uninterrupted night's sleep. I had slept for a while, but then had lain wide awake for hours just staring into the dark, trying to work through the maze of puzzles in my mind. Having no way to vent my anguish, I yearned to lash out at everything around me until grief and rage were swallowed by sheer exhaustion. All that I had ever prayed for was deliverance, but I knew something inside me had snapped as fury drowned all logic. God, how I wished sometimes that I was not so analytical...

I had long since finished my baguette and was draining the last of my cappuccino, whilst perusing the daily paper at the kitchen table. I suddenly felt the muscles of my stomach tighten. Apparently the police were now devoting new resources to the hunt for the serial killer who had already claimed four known victims (the last of which being Nikki). I was still not sleeping well, as black thoughts were currently weighing heavy on my mind. I wished that last night had just been a bad dream and not the very real nightmare that I was now embroiled in. I felt on edge and a little panicky as yet another wave of helpless fury washed over me. I felt as though I was living in a goldfish bowl, with police watching my every move... but it may have just been my paranoia? I had no way of knowing as my sensibilities were now blunted beyond all hope.

My nerves were as taut as wires. I longed for steadiness and serenity but instead found myself trapped within this city full of broken dreams. I felt so demoralised and weary, just a shred of hope for me remained, but I would cling to that.

Maybe I should just get away; start a new life abroad as there was nothing here for me now. I felt like an extra in 'Groundhog Day'. It was just the same old story being repeated

75

a million times and me crying through my dreams.

A breath of melancholy fluttered my eyelids closed for a brief moment before I fell forward and started to cry. Once I started I found that I could not stop, the tears cascading down my face until my eyes throbbed and my throat ached. Something inside me had snapped as I felt myself squirm a little at my memories.

PM

It had got colder and greyer outside now and light rain was spreading a film of damp on the concrete surfaces below.

For the last hour I had sat, staring out of the window, watching the rain beat down on the window pane, trying to predict which droplet would reach the sill first. A silent portrait of misery, obviously I'd had more productive days, but I was grateful as the glittering beyond the glass had temporarily distracted me from my anger at the world.

I was still tired and edgy due to my lack of sleep, history being my cage, but I was trying to get my life back on track as best I could, though I sensed that my death might be the only way out...

One hand absently rubbed my rumbling stomach as I tried to decide what to do next. I knew that I should really try to eat something but my stomach was too knotted and my body too exhausted to contemplate the preparation and consumption of a meal. I found that the anxiety and distress of recent days had savaged any appetite that I may have previously had.

I decided to scan the newspaper for job classifieds but in truth I was in no particular rush to return to the slave trade just yet. I still had enough money in my bank account to last another twelve months, possibly a bit longer if I was frugal, so I knew that I would not be on skid row just yet. On finding nothing of interest in the Evening Standard I tossed it aside and reached for the remote control. On flicking the television to life I was greeted by a mincing guy attired in a pink suit, who flapped around and appeared to be some sort of expert on interior design. I had seen enough, but channel hopping just confirmed my already firmly held belief that daytime television was solely targeted towards doped up students and housewives sedated on Valium.

I had noticed the facetious turn of my mind moving closer and closer to the surface during the last year, and it was currently my only defence against the mounting depression and frustration that I felt.

I switched the television off and went to run a bath, stopping on the way to pour a glass of Shiraz and to place a compact disc in the stereo. The water gradually began filling the bath as the strains of Fleetwood Mac filled the apartment. God, I must be depressed as even the thought of Stevie Nicks failed to stir any erotic feelings within me.

Oh well, there has to be a first time for everything I suppose...

I sat the wine glass down by the side of the taps and stepped gingerly into the bath, gently testing the water with my toes before committing my full body to it. I thought I almost heard my body sigh with relief as the warm water ebbed over my tense and aching muscles. I felt the tension slowly ebbing away from me and my spirits lifted as I reclined, sipping the red wine and singing along to Tango in the Night. I could not help but note that one of us sounded distinctly off key...

Meanwhile the warm water felt luxurious, like a million tiny fingers massaging my skin, easing every ounce of tension from me. The water felt silken as it flowed against my skin, caressing and lapping the contours of my naked body. As I lay there motionless, letting the hot water cascade over me, sloughing away all remnants of stress, I wondered why life could not always feel as good as this?

CHAPTER 11

THE SESSION

It was once again time for the weekly counselling session with my counsellor: Ms Duvall or Samantha as she preferred that I called her. I had reluctantly dragged myself away from the sanctuary of my apartment and was now sat in the waiting area outside Samantha's office. I perused the stack of dated magazines and daily newspapers. The latter of which all seemed to focus on the serial killer hysteria that was currently (and I suppose inevitably) sweeping the city.

I was a mass of contradictory feelings regarding the mass coverage as half of me was wanting to read more, whilst the other half loathed the gratuitous headlines that I now found myself squarely confronted with. Perhaps ignorance was bliss? Fortunately a decision did not need to be made on my part as just then the door to Samantha's office sprang open and I was ushered inside. I dropped the periodical that I had been clasping, back into the magazine rack and headed towards the unlocked door. Once inside the room I noted that Samantha looked very alluring today. Unusually her long red hair was worn down, so now a glossy cascade of burgundy flowed over her shoulders and down her back. Her pale smooth skin was lightly powdered and her wide hazel eyes bore the tiniest hint of make-up, whilst her slender figure was encased in a figure hugging charcoal Toscano Jacket, Latina classic long skirt and white silk blouse. I could not help but notice that her breasts, although not particularly large, were pressing purposefully against the soft fabric of her top. Her impressive outfit was completed and set off by a pair of shiny black leather kitten heeled Jimmy Choo shoes. She looked extremely elegant. I had never seen her so 'dressed up' before and hence I was quite taken aback by the vision that now stood before me.

There was no doubting that she was attractive but until this moment I had always been more aware of her erudite mind, personality and sensitivity, than her tall, slim and graceful body.

She smiled at me and gestured that I should take a seat. She remained as stoical and as unruffled as ever and I felt an irresistible urge to mirror her smile and warmth. She walked round to her desk and filled two cups from the coffee percolator, offering me one. I smiled a thank you. Grasping the cup like a trophy I took a gulp. The coffee hit my parched throat and kick-started my tonsils, for which I was grateful.

No matter how many times I had been here, I had never failed to be impressed by Samantha or her office. The office was vast.

Certificates adorned the walls and sat in frames upon the top of her broad oak desk, obviously a testament to her excellent credentials (well either that or she had obtained them from some dubious website)?!

Two plush leather chairs and a variety of potted plants sat upon the luxuriously soft thick pile carpet that when walked upon felt like you were gliding on a bed of feathers.

Samantha was equally impressive, not only beautiful but intelligent and intuitive. She was exceptionally gifted at her job (in my humble opinion) and had incredible patience and understanding. It had taken weeks, even months before she had managed to eventually worm her way through all of my defences and through the barricades of my mind to begin to unravel and attempt to heal the thirty years of pain and hurt. I surely must have driven her to distraction at the beginning but she never once let it show. Equally her eternal optimism drove me crazy at first, but now it felt reassuring for someone to have such faith and belief in me, and understanding of me. When Samantha spoke she was all affability, charm and tender empathy. Her support and advice had always been unwavering and wholehearted, whilst remaining wholly professional at all times.

I knew that my mind had been severely damaged by past events and traumas but I still had enough self-awareness to know that I needed to be helped and that these sessions were the only real way forward for me. I realised that I had to try to be more optimistic, that the traumas and their effects would hopefully pass with time.

I felt sure that with the right counselling the walls of my mind could be breached and the issues that formed them confronted head on. I was sure that sooner or later the barriers would all be broken down and I could confront the demons that presently made me such an emotional cripple. I desperately needed to stop my mind shutting off at stressful times, leading me to not being able to recollect certain periods of time or events that had just occurred: to stop crawling into myself and shutting out the rest of the world. I had noticed that the blackouts were becoming more frequent which was an obvious cause for concern for both Samantha and myself. Was it due to the added stress? The anxiety? Or perhaps it was the heady mixture of pills and alcohol?

The questions remained unanswered as I placed the coffee cup and saucer back on the desk in front of me and reclined in the plush leather chair.

Samantha pressed the record button on the cassette recorder and then walked back to her desk, before ensconcing herself in the black leather chair opposite me.

She picked up her notepad and pen as I took a deep breath and deliberately tried to focus my mind away from Samantha's long shapely nylon clad legs, to which it had drifted. I wanted to loosen up and let my thoughts and opinions just flow freely in front of her. I longed to share the burden I felt.

'A problem shared is a problem halved'…or so the saying goes (although in my experience the reality was the problem was then doubled as you then had two people worrying over the same dilemma).

Samantha's eyes met mine. She smiled luminously.

It was a radiant smile, a smile that took me with it.

I inhaled as I shifted down in my seat.

"How have you been since our last session Jamie?" Samantha enquired.

I replied that I'd had better weeks and then proceeded to tell her, in exaggerated detail… as all men do, about Nikki, the murder(s), the police visit and subsequent interview. Only once did she raise an eyebrow, other than that her expression remained fixed with her obviously well-practised confident façade intact. I was quite surprised as surely it could not be every day that a client marched into the office and informed her that they were the prime suspect in a murder enquiry?!

With rapt attention Samantha jotted copious notes as the tape machine whirred behind us. Her questions were set in conversational tone, rather than challenging and I sensed that she was starting to draw her own yet unvoiced conclusions from analysing my statements, gestures and every intricate piece of body language. She then leaned over and stared at me utterly engrossed as I spoke.

Had she read something in my eyes?

The hour flew by as I spoke and Samantha listened intently and sympathetically, only briefly our roles being reversed. I found Samantha's company curiously soothing and strangely comforting, like a warm gentle blanket on a cold night. Samantha was multi-faceted. Her combination of charm and intelligence was very disarming and alluring, especially as most of the time my life felt unbearable with happiness but a distant memory.

Some of my traumas were buried so deep that I felt they might even take years to unearth. I felt too unsettled and needed to get things back into perspective although on dark days sometimes I felt that the pattern was set and could never be broken. How I longed for deliverance from my pain, as I was sick of being damaged goods and wanted my life back and to live a fuller richer life that was emotionally fulfilled.

One day hopefully I could rejoin the rest of the world. The people I witnessed handling their emotions and setting out to mould their own bright futures. Each day I carried the blame but I no longer wanted to be a dysfunctional loser and a bleeding martyr!

I knew that the only way to survive the pain was to meet it head on. I was smart... I had dreams... I could make them come true.

I did feel somewhat of a lighter burden by the time the session concluded. It reconfirmed to me that these appointments were a necessary step in the right direction... albeit it at present, a slow one. Just hearing a familiar friendly voice once again made me feel a bit better and certainly more assured. In a world where no-one had ever cared, Samantha was indeed a tower of strength to me. Obviously just talking was helping me and I was secretly pleased to have the company as I had almost become a recluse of late, through no fault of my own. Any listener would have sufficed at present as after my marriage break up 'friends' had just stopped coming round.

I had no idea why, as surely I was the victim?

Samantha scribbled something in her diary and tapped piles of forms together before casting them to one side and escorting me to the door of her office. She exuded confidence and charm. A cute smile played on her lips and a sparkle lit her eyes as she took my hand, held my arm and bid me goodbye, inserting the appropriate support and encouragement. She was probably the only person in my life to have never failed me. Some debts could never be repaid (it was early days though as everyone betrayed me at some point).

I felt that I owed her a debt of gratitude though I had to wonder if secretly she did not get sick of being so patient and understanding. Mind you, they do say that the shrinks are secretly more screwed up than their patients don't they?

"See you next week, and take care of yourself. You must not lock yourself away. If you have any problems or if things are getting too much for you, you have my telephone number on the business card, so do not be afraid to use it."

I was touched by her concern and as I bade her good day, my smile turned genuine as I thanked her and said that I would not (I noted that my voice sounded hoarse and throaty from the previous hour's dialogue).

With that I left Samantha's office and began to descend the narrow spiral staircase until I reached the pavement below.

I felt slightly more optimistic but still somewhat bemused. I knew that I had to suck in my grief, dry my tears and march back into life's fight, but still my head was full of puzzles. I just wished that I could calm the confusion crashing about inside my head and to let sleeping dogs lie as all I could see was life's inconsistencies and the increasing chinks in my armour. For too long I had wallowed in despair, in a life gone forever, so I knew that it was now time to move on.

I planned to head back to my apartment but I knew that I had to pick up a few groceries and toiletries from town first.

Oh, the rock 'n' roll party animal lifestyle I led, never a dull moment...

As I stepped out onto the street I looked up at the silver sky and gazed out at infinity as the cacophony of noise around me assaulted my senses. Taxi drivers, whose cabs were loaded with summer tourists, were beeping their car horns at other vehicles that were sat static at traffic lights, that had long since turned green , whilst on the pavements restless children screamed and squawked, like demented parrots, whilst their parents remained somehow oblivious ...or just not caring. Whatever happened to the old adage of children being seen but not heard? It was at times like these that I felt that abortions should be compulsory as opposed to an option.

The shadows of the lampposts that crowded the roads fell upon me as I kicked my way through the litter covered pavement that was strewn with food containers and packaging from every fast food outlet imaginable. London had been this way for many years now partly due to the influx of immigrants and tourists that treated London like their personal fly tipping site and partly due to the respective local councils removing the street litter bins during the IRA's long running terror campaign. Was that still going? I recalled that they went from the IRA to the 'Real IRA', but they had been relatively quiet of late.

I pondered if they were now onto the 'New improved IRA'... they seemed to re-package themselves more often than the leading soap powders these days.

God I was feeling melancholy again...

I had only just left Samantha's office with what had then been a glimmer of renewed hope, but unfortunately the streets and people of London were not conducive to positive thought or a contented frame of mind. It truly was a godforsaken place, a complete concrete jungle where most of the inhabitants were feral and lawless. The capital was teeming with vermin, both of the rodent and of the human variety.

It never used to be this way.... did it?

As I pounded the pavement, crunching upon the dead and withered leaves and puddles of broken glass, I pondered where and when our society had gone so terribly wrong. As my gaze travelled along the backdrop of brick walls covered in graffiti and boarded up houses, I wallowed in disgust and loathing. How I yearned to leave the enveloping haze of the capital behind me.

The taut blue sky was clear of rain now, so I decided to walk home as I did not fancy being packed into a tube train as it felt akin to being a sardine in a tin (as even cattle had more luxurious travelling conditions than London's commuters these days).

On top of the extreme overcrowding I knew full well that there were bound to be delays or cancellations due to some outlandish excuse that only rail companies seemed to be able to get away with. (If their excuses became any more bizarre or far fetched I felt sure that it would only be a matter of time before Mulder and Scully would be called upon to investigate).

It would only take me an hour maximum to walk home and it would provide great exercise and a good chance to mull things over and hopefully clear my head (and to enhance my currently sombre mood).

I intended to nip into a few shops on the way back for the essentials that I needed. As I was useless in the kitchen I tended to live off microwave meals these days, since my wife took flight, so I would need to stock up on some of those and some milk (as I could not abide black coffee). I must remember to pop into the off-licence as well, as I was clean out of spirits. Not that I should really be drinking with the medication I was on, but what the hell, you only live once (thankfully) and besides I needed something to calm me down and stun my feelings.

There were now only vague distant figures on the pavement, yet I felt as if I were being watched. If anyone was following me I felt sure that I would have been able to spot them, so was it just my damned imagination that was troubling me?

As I trod the littered pavement I let my thoughts drift back to my memories of distant nostalgia, the images dark and remote as if blurred by shadows, like a film reel of my life playing inside my head...

I could not help but think that if it were ever to be screened that it would definitely be an 18 certificate, if it got passed by the censorship board at all. With that much tragedy I felt sure that I would be giving Woody Allen a good run for his money.

I drew in a deep breath that tasted of petrol and smoke. How my senses cried out for the fresh air of the countryside as I could not help but wallow in regret as I looked despairingly around me at the bleakness the capital projected... grey buildings, grey sky, grey paving slabs and even greyer people (that were unremittingly ordinary and appeared to live their lives via daily soap opera and 'reality TV' fixes).

Surely there had to be more to life than this?

The pain in my heart was becoming unbearable and I felt totally despondent, but all my tears were shed.

As I continued walking the mutter of the traffic was drowned out by the sound of police sirens wailing in the distance. I silently prayed to the gods to numb my awareness whilst my senses struggled to flee what had been done to me... but seemingly it was all to no avail as the tension I had expelled during my therapy session had now returned double-strength. I desperately needed a distraction, as I was finding it more difficult to care, about myself or about others. Faces from my past blurred together or were forgotten completely, with my own life being the only constant.

I tried to suppress the feelings, the sense of isolation and the utter solitariness in a world where everyone else had someone, but it was to no avail as the bitter sight of so many couples whilst I had no-one ate away at me like a cancer.

Goddammit, if only humans had a self destruct button, or we could escape into our dreams...

I was not picky; either would have been acceptable to me...

Just then my thoughts were jarred by the screech of tyres as a driver had stamped hard on the brake and skidded his car onto the stretch of road ahead of me. The car careered into a lamp-post, the impact with which crumpled the bonnet like tinfoil and shattered the windscreen. The spider's web of glass nailed to a blaze of sunlight.

As I drew level with the wreckage I had too much on my mind to pay more than a cursory glance but as the driver stumbled out (seemingly unharmed) of the concertinaed car, it re-confirmed to me that life was no lottery, instead our fates were already pre-determined.

I assumed that the gods had already chosen to forsake me...

CHAPTER 12

BREAKTHROUGH

Detective Inspector Ross stood behind his desk, in front of the office window, hands thrust deep inside his tweed jacket pockets, whilst staring down at his faded loafers that were more of a testament to comfort than style. His trousers and shirt were crumpled as he had been up all night going through the case notes with a fine- toothed comb. This case was all too important to him, so he knew that he could not afford for there to be any doubt, slip- ups or ramifications later on down the line. He just hoped that his judgement was not infallible and his decisions untainted by impulse.

He had the blinds rolled up and sunlight was streaming into the room. He stood basking in the brightness before eventually leaving the window and returning to his desk where he glanced down to the framed photographs of his wife and two teenage daughters.

His face was pale and drawn and his lips twisted as his mind raced. He was set to brief the investigation team in less than an hour and he was sure that what he was planning to do with the inquiry was the correct course of action. He was not to be dissuaded as he trusted his instincts and he desperately wanted this offender put behind bars as soon as possible, preferably with the key thrown away. He was tired of notifying next of kin, whilst the waiting press packs bayed like jackals for his blood, and news crews circled like ravenous vultures overhead. He knew that he would have to be guarded in his words to them (whilst reciting an eloquent plea for vigilance and assistance) at this afternoon's impending press conference.

His eyes were fully concentrated on the typed document in front of him. He had now received the forensic information back on the Nikki Chandler enquiry and had, on his desk, a profile from a noted criminal psychologist that stated the perpetrator was more likely than not to be a professional white male, aged twenty-five to forty-five years of age, who has above average intelligence but who will probably have had a problem with authority figures in the past. He was likely to have good knowledge of the local area though socially he would feel isolated and may have a juvenile record. Maybe there was something in this psychology lark after all? he mused.

He drew a breath of relief as all the pointers from the psychologists profile had reiterated the direction the forensic evidence and his own instincts (call it a copper's nose) had led him. The theory that he had come up with a while ago he was now fully prepared to commit to. He had applied to the court for a court order to see the suspect's medical and psychiatric reports and felt confident that the warrant would soon be issued. Damned patient confidentiality…It wasted so much time and caused so much added paperwork.

This arrest would be a real feather in his cap, he mused. It had been established beyond all reasonable doubt that all four known murders were undeniably linked with the same modus operandi, and although there was little or no DNA or forensic evidence found at the first three crime scenes, the fourth was a veritable treasure trove. He, Detective Inspector Ross, felt assured that the pattern of the crimes, the forensic evidence and the victims' profiles all led to one man, his suspect. He was as still and silent as a statue as his eyes travelled over the victims' photographs. He then once again glanced down at the interview transcript made by Detective Sergeant Armstrong and Detective Constable Regan, before shuffling the papers together and tossing them aside. He felt sure that his prime suspect would crumble under pressure, but would need handling with kid gloves whilst he was being drawn into the net. He had never felt entirely comfortable with predicting how anyone would react to a given situation but he was not a man to accept or recognise defeat and he was not about to start now.

His thoughts lingered as a smile crept slowly into the corners of his mouth but leaving his eyes untouched.

He knew that next came the battle of wits, and wills…

Detective Inspector Ross got set to summon his squad together for the briefing as he wished to brief his team as regards the imminent arrest and the line of questioning, based on the psychological report that he wished them to pursue. He was aware that with little or no direct evidence to the suspect, especially on the first three murders, that they would have to take full advantage, capitalizing on any and every weakness the suspect showed them. He suspected that he might need to unearth a motive and further incriminating evidence to satisfy the (CPS) Crown Prosecution Service. His intention was to obtain warrants for the arrest and search and once issued to grab their target in an early morning dawn raid, whereupon they could do a full search, ripping the place apart, looking under floorboards, behind the bath panel, the toilet cistern, bin cupboard... everywhere.

In his experience many murderers and serial killers tended to keep a trophy or souvenir of their crimes (or at the very least store cuttings from newspapers). Those were what he was hoping to find. He knew that he had to act swiftly though as he did not want the suspect getting wind of his imminent arrest and destroying crucial evidence. He knew that the suspect was already quite jumpy from what he had read on the interview transcript and his own discussions with the investigating officers.

If all went as he imagined it would be a major boost to his murder squad's morale and make up for the many days lack of a straight night's sleep. He went over to the window whilst sucking on a cigarette and looked out at the incident room, which was a quiet hub of activity. He had never seen a team work with that much intensity, dedication and fervour as on this case. He felt very proud of them, as some had not been home for days. That would not stop him giving them a little subtle browbeating though, just to keep them on their toes, as he fully believed that a little discipline never did anyone any harm.

Most of the officers were thumbing stacks of documents piled high upon their respective desks, whilst the remainder stared intently into their computer screens and frantically tapped away at their individual keyboards. He could not help but wonder as to what ever happened to the days when officers used to pound the beat and build up a network of informants to solve crimes.

The whole job nowadays seemed to be totally Information Technology driven. How he secretly pined for that bygone era.

He snapped his mind away from the thought and back to the modern policing methods. He wanted to make sure nothing went wrong with the arrest and prosecution. He did not want anyone doubting his efficiency and he did not want the slime ball getting off on a mere technicality. With such a high profile case he had to ensure that all the i's were dotted and all the t's were crossed. With the nation's media watching, and secretly willing him to fail, he could not afford any slip-ups. He knew that the gloves were off and he was damned if he would lose. He sensed that he was infallible, but he hoped that the momentary pangs of triumph he was feeling in his stomach were not overly premature as at the end of the day it was his judgement call and ultimately his head upon the chopping block. He shook the thought from his mind as he knew that to lose hope was to admit defeat. He was sure that the forensic findings more than made up for the lack of direct witnesses to the crimes.

He removed a new pack of cigarettes and a lighter from his jacket pocket and placed them on his desk whilst he smoothed back his steel grey thinning hair. He looked pregnant with beer as he tugged at his belt, which had inserted itself between two layers of fat.

'I really must get down the gym…well either that or start buying bigger belts,'…he thought inwardly.

He watched one of his officers uncap a black magic marker and begin to write something on the white board that housed the victims' photographs and personal details. He seemed oblivious to being observed (so much for all coppers having a sixth sense).

He attempted to gather his thoughts and went through the details that he was about to relay in his mind. The next step would be to gratify his expectations of a positive result, but he knew that he would have to prepare the ground carefully first. He had a plan and he felt quite confident about following it to its bitter conclusion. The unnervingly frustrating days were hopefully finally at an end and he was now prepared to go where angels had previously feared to tread.

A glimmer of cunning lit his eyes as he cleared his throat, straightened his tie and prepared himself to address and mobilize his assembled troops.

CHAPTER 13

BROKEN

I found myself lying wide-awake despite a desperate need for more sleep. Horrors had flashed in the dark as with nightfall had come a sense of foreboding that refused to let me relax. I turned on the bedside lamp and sat up in bed. My neck and shoulders were sore and ached from being bent in the wrong position. My back was achy and stiff whilst my body, as ever, was rigid with tension.

I got up slowly and stretched, slipping my legs down and perching on the side of the bed. I had neither been eating nor sleeping well as a welter of emotion had swirled inside me. I felt bereft and bewildered, so most of the time I had remained in bed, huddled beneath the duvet. I did not fully remember my dreams but I had wept until my eyes had almost swollen shut. I only knew tortured sleep and it showed in my eyes, with the dark shadows around them I was fast turning into a human panda. I felt totally drained, as if I had been put through the emotional wringer. I just felt so weak and insignificant. Panic had given way to dull despair; it was as if my entire world existed within the confines of these four walls. I stood up and drew the curtains to let the daylight in.

I noted that the morning was overcast, with the sky being the same grey as the paving stones outside. Any sun had long since disappeared and rain had begun to fall lightly as I gazed out of the window and observed the flowing traffic below. I looked up and saw leaves fluttering in the wind like disembodied spirits...

My galloping thoughts were interrupted as the letter box clattered as the daily paper thudded on to the door mat. I rose from the window sill and wandered to the front door.

Upon picking up the paper I unfolded it and plunging myself into the kitchen chair, began to read. Within seconds I felt myself breaking out into a sweat and felt stabbing pains that seemed to be piercing my heart. Hot and pained inside I could not stop the tears and for a while I just wept with anguish and heartache. I dabbed at my eyes with tissues, my stomach churning as I stared down at the newspaper. I had to restrain myself from screaming aloud as there was a front page splash on the hunt for the serial killer and a large photo of Nikki (who looked beautiful) was printed alongside the other three murder victims. Strangely, they all looked familiar, but aside from Nikki and one woman who I recognised as working, or had worked, at my local supermarket, I failed to place how or from where I knew the other two women. Perhaps I had just seen them locally or recalled their photographs in papers previously? I mused.

Recollection wise, I was vague about so many things at present.

I just wished the hidden memories would come flooding back to me, but perhaps it was a blessing that they did not as I knew from bitter experience that some thoughts were undeniably destructive and crushing. Until I knew the answers I would have to battle on but I wished that I had something more tangible to cling to...

I had not eaten in almost forty-eight hours but I still had no appetite. I was still smoking like the proverbial chimney and drinking like the proverbial fish... seemingly, old habits died hard.

I breathed deeply as I tried to relax but inside I still felt hollow and bruised, unable to dislodge the dark thoughts from my brain. I had been through pain, both mental and physical, before so I was aware that there was no quick fix. There were so many voices inside my head now, screams and prayers, rage and pain...sometimes even blame.

I felt on the verge of hysteria even though I was accustomed to being alone with only my morbid regrets for company. My mind was a whirling torrent of emotion. I just could not understand why my life had ended up this way as I was smart, always top of my class at school and I had such dreams and ambitions. I could have made them all come true, so what went wrong? Feeling the pain inside, I shut my eyes, my brow furrowed and my heart beat so hard that it hurt. I felt that I had been pushed to the limit emotionally and was now unsure of my next course of action.

Just where the hell did my life go from here?

I ran my hand across my chin and felt that my face was dirty with stubble, so I walked to the bathroom and removed the razor and shaving foam from the cabinet above the sink. Whilst staring into the mirror, I pumped a fair amount of the silky white foam into the palm of my hand and lathered up my neck and face so that I now resembled Father Christmas after a highly successful weight watchers campaign. I slid the razor along the craggy contours of my face as small traces of blood began to mingle with the soft foam. Just why was it impossible to wet shave without nicking yourself at least once, no matter how careful you were?

I finished off shaving and stepped into the shower. The warm jets felt like pieces of shimmering silk and were a more than welcome relief to my previously tension bound body. The water touching my face felt like a million tiny massaging fingers and eased me instantly.

After taking a long shower I dried myself with a towel and changed into a David Lee Roth Tee-shirt and tight blue stonewashed jeans. I felt parched, so I headed towards the kitchen to make some strong coffee to kick start my day. I filled the kettle and switched it on as I popped a couple of slices of medium sliced white bread into the toaster.

I really had to try and eat something.

I was emotionally drained and still felt desperately alone.

Normally I did not mind my own company (as I was more interesting than most of the people I met) but the recent events were deeply troubling me, so much so that I currently felt stark and desolate, whilst images from the past prickled like a needle in my mind. I just hoped that boredom was not having a detrimental effect on my sanity...

My thoughts disentangled as suddenly the telephone rang, startling me back to reality. I was not even aware that I had momentarily closed my eyes but the sound of the telephone ringing had immediately snapped them open. For those few magical seconds I had imagined that I had just awoken from a really bad dream.

Unfortunately this was not the case.

"Hello," I said abruptly, whilst I tried desperately to gather my scattered senses.

"Good morning sir, my name is Duncan. I work for Ever-Glaze Windows. I am not trying to sell you anything. The reason for the call is that we are in the process of opening a new showroom locally and we are looking for show houses that we could use in exchange for a fantastic discount on any work done. I was wondering if I could interest you in obtaining a free quote. Obviously there is no obligation to purchase anything. We currently have a representative in your area who..."

Duncan had not sensed my growing impatience, so I hung up, cutting him off mid spiel. He may not have been a cowboy but I could have sworn I heard his spurs jangling at the other end of the phone line. Great timing... tele-sales callers, just what I needed... they certainly knew how to piss in your cornflakes.

The ache in my heart grew more intense as once again my thoughts wandered to the dark recesses of my mind and tugged despairingly.

Just what was it that I was trying to remember?

Unfortunately you cannot put your arms around a memory, and even the home that I once thought of as being spacious and tastefully decorated now seemed dim and bare, as if my own private prison cell.

As I was becoming increasingly restless, I decided to fill some time by checking my emails and scanning the internet. Chat rooms were always a great way to lose yourself for a few spare hours, as you could be anyone that you wanted to be. I hit the enter key to turn the screen saver off. Sadly Courtney Cox-Arquette disappeared from view. At a prompt I typed in my user name and password and entered the wondrous world of the web. Firstly I clicked on to my hotmail account, sorting the mail by date order before slowly beginning to scroll through them. It turned out that there was nothing of any real interest though as my inbox mainly consisted of the obligatory unsolicited emails, porn and 'spam' messages, along with the odd gig and cinema listing. Not a single so called friend or ex-colleague had emailed me to enquire as to how I was doing (and people say the sense of community is dead)?

Hours passed as I surfed cyber space, accumulating a number of different identities and personas in various chat rooms along the way. It was the virtual reality equivalent of the dressing up box that I had when I was a kid. My hopeless misery was temporarily forgotten as I loved being able to visualise being anyone but me. The bullied scared abused child ceased to exist for those few brief but glorious moments, as I dressed up in my mum and dad's old clothes and unabashed fantasy thankfully overtook my grim and stark reality. The sanctuary never lasting too long though, as it had to abruptly cease before my father returned home from the pub. If I were to be caught I would feel his wrath and the inevitable sting of his fist.

Dressing up was sissy and only a thing girls did, apparently...

PM

It was a balmy evening so I sat reclining in a white plastic garden chair out on my small balcony, drinking and smoking whilst looking over the city, which appeared to come alive at night. The nearby strains of my radio spilled out through the night air but I reached over and turned down the volume a notch, as I had not realised quite how late it now was as night had fallen quickly. As the light faded, shadows crept across the veranda and in the growing dark I watched the shapes of people flow by below.

Some were loud and boisterous and were holding on to each other for support (obviously the worse for alcohol) whilst others moved along with a lot more purpose. I assumed, possibly wrongly, that they must have been night workers just going to or from their graveyard shifts. Down below amongst the blurred roar of traffic, a frustrated taxi driver noisily sounded his horn at drunken jaywalkers.

Staring into space, I cast my eyes heavenwards through the smoke touched sky, towards the irregular moon and the twinkling stars, which peeked through the cover of the night. I could feel the breath of the night air on my face as I instinctively blinked back the tears that had welled in my eyes and tried to dismiss my stench of failure. It felt lonely being me. It was a shame that I inhabited a world in which it was unpardonable that anyone could be without a partner as I was left with an evening of brooding solitude. I tried to crush those feelings as I tapped out a cigarette from the packet of Marlboros and upon lighting it blew perfect smoke rings into the night sky. It seemed no matter how old I was the enjoyment of that particular trick never diminished. Perhaps it was just a guy thing? As the saying goes, 'little things please little minds...'

I was either getting tired or was now half drunk, or a combination of both, as I could feel my eyes closing as I took another sip of red burgundy. Even though the September night was mild I still found myself shivering slightly, added to which, I was beginning to get maudlin again so decided I should soon retire to bed to try and obtain some much needed and long overdue slumber (as I knew that otherwise I would be useless in the morning).

Unfortunately, I did not turn off my bedside lamp until way past 4am after an aborted attempt to read the latest Stephen King novel ended in abject failure. With depression hanging over me, I just could not absorb the pages that I was attempting to read. I obviously had too much other stuff cluttering up my mind. To sleep seemed an impossible ambition; I doubted I would ever sleep again. How I wished that humans came equipped with a delete button sometimes.

As I lay on my back in bed staring into the darkness, my mind became a raging torrent of thoughts and neurotic fear. I was once again feeling emotionally drained and all alone. Some things were almost inescapable, but I just wished it all would stop. I felt as if my life were a roller-coaster and I just wanted to get off and let someone else have a turn as I had become dizzy and tired of the white-knuckle ride.

It was not so long ago, when I had met Nikki that I had felt so different, like a phoenix rising from the ashes... albeit briefly.

I was sure that she had been the one for me as she felt like my soul mate and kindred spirit. I knew that I had not known her for very long and most people would dismiss it as being a one-night- stand, but to me it was a paradise that I would remember in my heart forever. I only hoped that in a different realm we would meet again...

I wished that I could clear my head and get the jumble of thoughts and contradictions, which were currently in my mind, into some semblance of order. Endless questions filled my mind and I was somewhat frightened by the answers.

Upon trying to sleep I found that I just could not settle. The duvet had been kicked to the middle of the floor, the pillows pounded into submission and my legs entwined around the bottom sheet as I tossed and turned in several failed attempts to get comfortable. Even though I was only attired in a white tee-shirt and boxer shorts I still felt hot, clammy and uncomfortable. Sweat was running into my eyes and poured from my brow, back and neck even though the bedroom window was ajar and a cool breeze was floating in. What do they say? 'No rest for the wicked'...perhaps there was some truth to that after all as some nights I felt like I had died or at least some part of me deep inside was dying. Fighting the escalating depression, I sat up in bed and reached for the half empty glass of red wine, which sat perched precariously on my bedside cabinet. I took a healthy gulp in a vain attempt to numb the pain and the voices in my head that were now overtaking me. Feeling the rhythmic throbbing of my temple, I took a deep breath and wiping my brow, tried to settle back down. I had just closed my eyes again when my brow furrowed as I thought that I heard voices, footsteps and hurried movements outside. I wondered drowsily why someone was padding down the corridor but I dismissed it as people setting off early for work in an attempt to avoid the gridlock of rush hour traffic congestion.

I had just turned over in bed and plumped the pillows beneath me when there was a good solid knock at the door. I tried to gather my senses as I looked across at the glowing alarm clock. It told me it was 4:40am. This understandably irked me considerably and I shook my head in disbelief, as I was now over-tired, aching and extremely irritable. I sighed loudly, deeply... Just who the hell would call at such an ungodly hour?

Again, knocking, louder this time and more prolonged as their fists collided with the front door. The sound of the hammering on the door was obviously drawing my attention towards the hallway and I could sense the wood almost splintering with the force. I thought I even saw the door bulge inwards as the insistent pounding rattled the apartment door on its hinges, which I felt sure, would soon pop.

Just what the hell was going on?

"Who is it?" I called out angrily.

"It's the police, open up." Their tone was hard, impatient and demanding. Even in my frazzled state, there could be no doubting their sense of urgency.

After a moment of confusion I sat up in bed, feeling dizzy. My stomach growled and churned, reminding me that I had not eaten since the previous day.

The effects of the alcohol led to me to stumble wearily to the hallway. I blinked and struggled to focus as my head was spinning. I slipped the chain on the door and cautiously opened it. Still straining my eyes, I eventually recognised two of the unwelcome visitors in front of me from our previous encounters and taking a deep breath I un-slipped the chain.

As the assembled officers stepped through the door, Detective Sergeant Armstrong looked me straight in the eye. His eyes were hard and unyielding and I noted his forehead was creased into a frown as he made little effort to hide his feelings of distaste towards me.

I could not understand why the hell did they keep bothering me?

I was not thinking clearly, with the consumption of alcohol I was definitely a bit slow on the uptake.

"Could you not have called at a more reasonable hour?" I uttered in a drunken slur, my voice shaking with anger.

There seemed to be a prolonged silence before a warrant was flashed in front of my face.

"We have a warrant for your arrest and giving authorization for us to search your premises. I need to make you aware of your rights. Jamie Allen, you are being arrested on suspicion of murder. You do not have to say anything, but it may harm your defence if you do not mention when questioned, something which you later rely on in court. Anything you do say may be given in evidence."

Detective Sergeant Armstrong spoke in the manner of a responsible person piously proud of doing their duty.

For a moment I froze as the officer's words had turned me cold all over, it was like a bad dream from which I was yet to awaken. I felt a spasm of apprehension yet was utterly furious with their intrusion.

"If you would like to put some clothes on sir, we can..."

I understandably felt incensed about being arrested and when my patience was no more I interrupted, rage and panic igniting me.

"This is absurd, I have not killed anyone. I loved Nikki. She was kind and caring and wonderful, why on earth would I want to kill a woman like that?!"

The steel in my spine had turned to mercury (at my mention of Nikki), the hardness and anger were gone from my voice and as I spoke it reflected only the weariness and sadness that I felt.

It did not make any difference though as the question hung in the air and received no reply or acknowledgement.

As the officers brushed past me into the living room, I kept a level stare but inside I was now scared and worried and beginning to sober up rapidly. As if a fly, I was chillingly aware of the web that I was now entangled in. As I looked around in confusion, I knew now that this was no dream I was engulfed in, but naked reality (even though the events just seemed so devoid of any rationality).

I felt physically and mentally wiped out but I tried to gather my thoughts as subconsciously my lips tightened and contorted in unspoken anger. I could not concentrate: too much wine, but I knew that I would have to be guarded with my words until I could speak with a solicitor, whom I was sure would get this whole mess straightened out.

The officers shot me an impatient look but I turned away.

A cold chill had settled over my spirit and the atmosphere inside my apartment was currently so intense that I almost felt physically sick. I had not eaten properly for days although I could now feel what felt like half a brewery swimming inside of me.

I felt worn down and defeated, with the hatred within my apartment currently so thick that I felt as if I were suffocating. My nerves had begun to hum and it prevented me from thinking clearly as I smelt their lust for blood.

I was accompanied to my bedroom to get dressed, which seemed to necessitate a flurry of discussion and a stream of vulgarity. The officers definitely took vicious pleasure in their jobs...

Once I was attired in my shirt, trousers and shoes I returned (accompanied) to the living room where I noted that police officers had started bagging and tagging my items from within the apartment. I did not see all of the items that they were planning to remove but I noted that Nikki's bracelet was now inside a see-through bag. Even more bizarrely were a bundle of newspapers. Surely they were not that short of chip wrappers at the police station I could not help but to ponder to myself.

My computer terminal was then disconnected and carried out, along with all my floppy discs in their carrying cases. My filing cabinets were rifled through with folders being tossed into waiting cardboard boxes, before being sealed.

The officers continued to go through my apartment like a plague of locusts. No draw was left un-emptied and no cupboard left intact. I could not believe that I was witnessing strangers tearing my home apart. Even the entire contents from my waste bin were now situated in the middle of the kitchen floor, whilst my clothes were strewn in a heap upon the carpet and my bedding stripped; (It looked as though Tracey Emin had just launched another exhibition of her works), I doubted that they were planning to do my laundry as it was not even wash day, so heaven only knows what they hoped to find.

My home now looked like it had been in the path of hurricane Annie. I stood momentarily dumbfounded as I could only stare, uncomprehendingly. The sight, so incongruous, that I blinked and rubbed my eyes, before looking again. I was unable to swallow my inner rage any longer and felt myself snap.

"I hope that you are planning to put all that stuff back where you found it," I bellowed.

The question was met with a grinned silence, so obviously I had received my answer. I snapped my jaw shut, swallowing my next sentence. I felt pure contempt for their pettiness and spite. I could sense the officers' dark gaze upon me but I did not meet their eyes. After a moment of muted unease, I shifted my stance to stare out of the window. I shook my head as a mixture of fear and anger ran through my mind. It was an uncomfortable and disorientating sensation, the alienation complete when I realised that I would wake up tomorrow to see myself in all of the newspapers and splattered across the television networks. The howling television and press packs had been baying for blood for weeks now and I was scared of what the consequences might be. I remembered that poor bastard the police had tried to stitch up on the Rachel Nickell case. Like him, would I too be a marked man even once, or should that be... IF... I cleared my name? I rolled my eyes as I bit back the urge to scream.

Did the police not realise how their incompetence destroyed innocent peoples' lives (as unfortunately the vast majority of the general public were foolish enough to believe everything that they were spoon-fed by the assorted media). I sucked in my cheeks, shaking my head as I felt frustrated, helpless and hollow with panic. I clenched my teeth tightly as I could see any hope of a fair trial going up in smoke. Only an occasional murmur now broke the silence, so I was terrified and froze in fear when handcuffs clamped my hands solidly behind my back. With what I sensed was a small measure of satisfaction Detective Sergeant Armstrong grabbed my arm and I was led down the twisting spiral staircase towards the waiting squad car. I noted that the morning was bright and the air felt crisp and cool on my skin. As I strode over the gravel which crunched underfoot, I breathed in the fresh morning air and just hoped that it was not the last time that I would be savouring it. I felt a bit stiff legged as I was frog-marched out, and I found that my eyes prickled as they were desperately trying to re-adjust to the growing daylight. The sensation of panic overwhelmed me, I had no desire to spend the rest of my days cooped up in some prison or mental institution, just because the police were too inept (or should that be too ignorant) to do their jobs properly.

I once again caught the scent of the morning as the early morning breeze ruffled my hair, whilst I was being unceremoniously bundled into the back of the waiting police car. Detective Constable Regan went round to the other side of the car and joined me in the back seat whilst Detective Sergeant Armstrong and another unidentified officer (with a face only a mother could love) occupied the front ones. As the car doors were slammed shut, I was a bit disconcerted to find myself shivering, but due to the ridiculousness of the situation I could not help but for my lips to curl into a rueful, sardonic smile (as my anger and disgust rose to the surface).

"Is there something amusing you sir?"

It was Detective Constable Regan who had snapped away from his disinterested stare and had spoken, his eyes darkening.

I felt self-conscious under his dark, cold and disapproving eye, but despite having become inflamed by the man I bit back the flippant reply that spring to mind: Only your dress sense.

I knew that he would not have seen the funny side of it.

The tightening of my lips was my only response, as anger steadily rose inside me, spreading heat all over my body.

The detectives remained silent for the rest of the journey, as did I.

I felt like a fattened calf being led to the slaughterhouse when ten minutes later we pulled up into the car park (at the rear of the now all too familiar police station). I attempted not to give a flicker of reaction, but I think my nerves gave me away. I was escorted into the station through the back door, with an officer holding either arm. I resisted the urge to do the hokey cokey.

Our footsteps echoed across the hard wood floor and up and an empty corridor that snaked off to (as yet) unknown territory.

We approached another officer seated behind a large wooden counter, who introduced himself to me as the custody sergeant and asked if I understood why I had been arrested. As his gaze passed over me, I nodded gravely, lowering my eyes. Struggling initially to get any words out, I eventually answered in the affirmative.

I was asked a number of mundane questions, such as name, address, date of birth and occupation. I answered absently, as I was already becoming disillusioned by the proceedings and had already spoken to too many sub-literate drones this morning.

"Would you like anyone notified of your arrest?"

"No."

I mouthed a sharp curse as I bit my lip in anger and dismay, as the only person who might have possibly given a damn about me was now lying on a mortuary slab and bizarrely, I was the one now being accused of putting her there. At that thought, I felt a single tear slip out, so I squeezed my eyes tightly shut.

My handcuffs were eventually removed and I instinctively rubbed at my aching and swollen wrists. I did a visual sweep of the area, before I was then 'patted down' by one of the uniformed officers (obviously looking for WMD). Once given the all clear I was then handed a copy of the 'codes of practice on detention' pamphlet to read.

Apparently the police were obliged to review my detention after six, fifteen and twenty-four hours to decide if it was necessary to continue to hold me in custody.

(I loathed the police with a passion after my teenage experiences with them, so I prayed that the matter would soon be cleared up and that I would not be here for the whole duration).

I gave up reading after a couple of lines as I was too fatigued to read or concentrate fully (and besides Pulitzer Prize winning material it was not).

Whilst still perspiring with rage, I felt myself twitch in agitation as vague currents of ghostly chill shimmered down the corridor and tickled the nape of my neck. The police station seemed cool, almost cold compared to the warm autumnal day outside, so I suspected that they had the air conditioning cranked up way too high.

Meanwhile, despite my obvious lack of enthusiasm, the custody sergeant continued with his requests that were as emotionless as his stare.

"Could you please empty your pockets sir and remove your watch, any jewellery, belt, tie and shoe laces."

I felt my brow knit but I did as I was instructed, although I was unable to remove my wedding band as it was on too tight. My fingers must have swollen up. I was not even sure why I still wore it, but I just could not bear not to, albeit on my right hand.

The sudden thought of my marriage added to the bitter resentment that I was feeling.

The custody sergeant logged all my possessions on a form attached to a clipboard, which he then turned towards me.

When he spoke, his voice was unruffled but firm.

"Can you read through the list and verify that all your possessions are listed. If you are satisfied that they are, please sign your name on the bottom of the form."

(Quite whose name he had expected me to sign, had he not told me to write my own, I could scarcely imagine).

The custody sergeant turned his empty stare on me and waited.

We locked gazes for a brief moment before I tore mine away.

I checked the list and found that all was in order, so as instructed I signed.

I half expected that Jeremy Beadle would pop out from behind a corner, microphone in hand and camera crew in tow.

Unfortunately they did not.

"Have you been read your rights?"

I replied that I had.

"Do you have legal representation that we could call or would you like to see the duty solicitor?"

As I only had a divorce lawyer, I replied that the latter would be fine.

His voice momentarily softened as his gaze moved over me.

"Do you have any special dietary requirements?"

I was sorely tempted to state: Caviar, Salmon and Jack Daniels, but I assumed that the joke had been done before, so I bit my lip and just responded in the negative.

As I stood there feeling like an extra on 'The Bill', the custody sergeant picked up the phone from its cradle, presumably to call the duty solicitor.

I noted that he gripped it tightly between his shoulder and ear, as he begun to write quickly on to the pad in front of him.

My stomach tightened in anticipation and my hand instinctively clamped tightly to it, as I tried unsuccessfully to remain calm.

My vision clouded for a moment, like a mental stutter. Feeling somewhat disorientated, I said that I needed to use the gents and was escorted to the bathroom to answer the call of nature. I noted that a 'Wet Floor' sign was pinned up upon the bathroom door, but as my bladder was now at bursting point it seemed more like an instruction than a warning. Thankfully though, I reached the urinal in time. After emptying my previously aching bladder and re-zipping my flies, I turned on the tap and filled the sink next to me. I removed my jacket and rolled up my sleeves.

A sheen of perspiration covered my forehead, so cupping my hands together I splashed cold water on my face in a bid to revive myself, as my head was still fuzzy from the alcohol that I had consumed in the wee small hours. Glancing at my reflection in the mirror I realised that for the past few days (if not longer) I had paid very little attention to my appearance. My hair was rough and tangled whilst my face was aged by anxiety. I noted that my eyes were shadowed by fatigue and disenchantment and I looked far beyond my years. I dried my face and hands on one of those awful coarse paper towels from the dispenser that was situated on the wall next to me. They were so abrasive that it felt as if I were was like rubbing myself with sandpaper.

My skin must have been secretly cursing me, and I knew that if I were to stay here much longer that I would be shopping for Oil of Olay upon my release.

On returning to the custody area I felt a tad better but my exasperation, impatience and resentment were beginning to re-emerge as I had never had been one to suffer fools gladly.

I closed my eyes briefly as I uttered a silent prayer as distant echoes of footsteps and voices carried along the narrow corridor, which was still cool from the air-conditioned breeze and that bought goose-bumps springing to my arms.

Just then the set of double doors swung open and a woman entered. She gave me no heed as she walked past but instead arrowed straight towards the custody sergeant, who in turn acknowledged her. I wondered if this was the duty solicitor. I kind of hoped she was as if I were to be stuck here for some time at least it would be nice to have some eye-candy.

I could not quite hear all of what she was saying to the custody sergeant but I noted that that her voice was rich, cool, quiet and confident. I thought that I may have even detected a subtle lilting Irish brogue. Her auburn hair was tied back in a ponytail and she was very smartly attired in a charcoal business suit. Her age was hard to predetermine but I guessed she was just slightly older than me, so possibly in her mid to late thirties. She had dazzlingly white skin, as if made of porcelain. Her features were striking and sharp, whilst her body was sensual and athletic.

I was suddenly aware of the tension and malaise within me as my pulse pounded in my neck. I straightened up and took a deep breath in an attempt to settle myself down, though I could still feel my body shaking badly.

The woman, who was still in conversation with the custody sergeant, glanced quizzically over at me. Her emerald eyes were shadowed in thought. She had a hard expression to read, so assuming that she was my solicitor, I was still no wiser as to her first impressions of me. I felt a mixture of annoyance and embarrassment as I gave a slow cautious gaze, my shoulders tensing in anticipation as I felt as though I was awaiting the hangman's noose. I muttered a curse under my breath.

Eventually she came over, shook my hand (she had a surprisingly firm grip) and introduced herself as Diane Keane, the duty solicitor.

I took another deep breath to mask my anxiety, as there was now a knot where my empty stomach had been.

Apparently I was entitled to consult with a solicitor privately, so minutes later we were seated alone in a private interview room as, pen poised over her notebook, Ms Keane took my details, asked about any previous run-ins that I had with the police and invited me to recount my version of events that had led up to the arrest.

Diane sat across from me and leaned over the table, seemingly urging me to confide in her as she fixed me with a smile, a look of sympathy. I met her gaze, keeping my voice soft.

Diane looked on silently and took notes as I spoke, giving the details she required. Although maladjusted, I wanted to be completely open with her, so I told her about my petty juvenile record, the theft and shoplifting charges that I had faced in my youth, my family life that had led me to becoming a runaway and a rent boy and having to live on my wits on the streets of London (having absconded from more children's care homes than I cared to recall). I felt my face reddening as I then told her of my weekly counselling sessions with Samantha (due to the mental breakdown I had suffered after my wife left me and took everything that was not nailed down), and my meeting Nikki and how great it had been, albeit for a cruelly short amount of time. I stressed to her that I was totally innocent and that if the case ever got as far as a trial that I would obviously be pleading 'Not Guilty'. With dehydration from the previously consumed alcohol and my nicotine addiction, I noted that my voice was fast becoming dry and hoarse. My tone was emotional as I choked back the bitter tears that had welled up deep within. I felt spied upon, caged by the anonymous room.

Ms Keane listened patiently to what I had to say, nodding but keeping her face impervious. Her concern, when she spoke, seemed genuine as she smiled back at me with just the correct amount of support and care. I noted that her eyes were wide with what I assumed was glinting curiosity.

I found the intensity of her personality compelling.

She listened in fascination, her expression sympathetic and encouraging, although I could not be sure of how much of what I was currently telling her that she actually believed (as some of it sounded far-fetched, even to my own mind). I looked over at Diane. Her eyes were on mine, waiting with a mixture of quiet interest and understanding that made me want to go on. Her compassion provided a touch of warmth, defrosting the chill that had settled over me.

When our conversation had finished and Ms Keane felt that she was now in possession of all the relevant facts she went silent, pensive…obviously thinking back over our conversation whilst checking through her handwritten notes.

"Do you know of anything or anyone that the police may call in evidence against you?"

"No," I confirmed with growing curiosity.

Diane said nothing for the moment, but her eyes were coming alive (sculpted eyebrows arching), as if relishing the forthcoming challenge. When she did speak her voice was calm and analytical, if somewhat guarded.

Meanwhile I had dread in my heart and could barely speak. I knew emotionally that I could never survive prison and just prayed inwardly that Ms Keane would be able to get this obvious misunderstanding sorted out. That was the only hope that I had left to cling to.

I felt myself relinquishing any control, however slim, I had previously held over the situation, and being a control-freak, I loathed the feeling.

I was informed that I could be detained in custody, without being formally charged, for up to a four day holding period as long as the police obtained ongoing warrants from a local magistrate. After that time I would be free to go should no charges be brought. While I tried to absorb the information I noted that it had almost gone silent, the only faint noise was the gush of cold air that spilled tirelessly from the vents.

At that precise moment there was a knock at the door.

I knew that it would only spell bad news, so I gazed down at my interlocked fingers, forcing myself to breath slowly, whilst Diane arose from her chair and went to the door. After a quick conversation Diane turned back to face me as the door closed softly behind her.

"The detectives would like the interview to commence soon. Would you be happy with that or is there anything else you need to discuss with me, to ask me, or that you need clarifying?"

"No, I am fine... well, at least as can be expected in the circumstances. Please just get me out of here."

As Diane met my eyes her expression was calm and open.

"I will do my best. Now, just tell the truth. Tell them the version of events as you told me. If they try to bully or pressurise you, I will step in. You have the right to answer 'no comment' to any or all of the questions. It is up to the police to prove your guilt as opposed to you having to prove your innocence, so remember that and do not let them browbeat you or attempt to bully you into a corner. Remember that they are intensively trained in interview techniques, so will try a variety of methods for getting you to drop your guard. You are known to the police, so they will try to twist everything you say and try to rattle you and get under your skin. Just remember to stay calm and composed. Try to remain focussed. Remember that you are innocent. I will assist you where needed, and as long as you were telling me the whole truth as you recall it, you should have nothing to worry about."

As her lips curved into a sympathetic smile, I noted that her lurch into enthusiasm was almost as sudden as her initial wariness had been.

I nodded cautiously as I allowed myself an instant of guarded relief. I noted that Diane's face was relaxed, eyes alert and interested as she continued to speak.

"If you would prefer, you could prepare a statement now,

setting everything you know out and once you have read it aloud in front of the tape recorder, you can decline to say anything beyond that."

I appreciated the thought.

I was deeply concerned about the rapidly spiralling events but I mulled the proposition over for an all too brief moment, before replying.

"No, I should be fine with answering their questions, as I do not want them to think that I have something to hide."

There was another knock on the door and upon receiving the appropriate response, the handle twisted and the door sprung open. Detective Constable Regan and Detective Sergeant Armstrong pushed through the door and entered the room (in a good dramatic fashion) as mentally I tried to cut through the tension and anticipation and prepare myself for what I knew would be an ongoing battle of wills. I was alternating hope and dreadful fear as the two officers lowered themselves into the chairs across from Ms Keane and myself. Their chairs scraped across the tiled floor as I noted that only a strong wooden table (with innumerable hairline scratches) now separated me from my opponents. The situation reminded me of the old chess club at school, but only this time the game had my freedom at stake.

Beneath the table a cold snake of fear had wound up through my body and I could feel my legs trembling uncontrollably. I pressed my knees together but they still shook, as my body mirrored my thoughts. I realised that as soon as the opportunity arose that the officers would insult and demean me, as I had been through all of this many times before…though, admittedly with not quite so much at stake.

The thought rebounded through my skull for what seemed like forever, causing a rolling nausea to engulf me briefly and led me to tighten my jaw. I took a deep, slow breath.

God, please do not let me throw up…

Both Ms Keane and myself were offered cups of tea or coffee, and myself a cigarette. I had craved a cup of coffee up until that moment but after noting the officers' wolf like smiles I was immediately on my guard. I felt like Little Red Riding Hood, all I needed was the bonnet. As a result, both Ms Keane and myself politely declined the offer of any refreshment.

Detective Constable Regan reached across and lifted two blank cassette tapes from the table at which we were seated. He individually removed the cellophane that encased them and then placed both tapes into separate compartments of the tape recorder perched at the end of the table nearest the wall. Detective Constable Regan pressed the record button and the cassette player kicked into life immediately. A faint hum and whirr filtered through the air of the interrogation room, like an expectant bee.

Detective Sergeant Armstrong was the first to speak.

"The date is the 8th September 2004, the time being 6:45am.

I am Detective Sergeant Armstrong. Also present are Detective Constable Regan, Mr Jamie Allen and his legal representative Ms Diane Keane…"

As anxious as I was I knew that I would have to be careful. My gut went cold as I exhaled. I glanced across at Ms Keane as Detective Sergeant Armstrong got into full swing and read me my rights. Obviously sensing that I was very nervous and agitated Diane gave me a reassuring smile. She looked very composed and assured as she sat there with her pen poised over the notebook, which was resting on her knee.

Detective Sergeant Armstrong was still droning on, in his now all too familiar neutral and nasal tone, but with my fatigue and raging hangover I was not taking it all in. I think that I had the beginnings of a migraine as pain was now shooting behind my eyes and temples. My gaze roamed up to the sullen grey walls of the interview room. I was far from thinking clearly, I could hear Detective Sergeant Armstrong's voice but a part of me just did not want to listen, as I still hoped that I was just in the middle of some terrible nightmare and at any moment I would snap out of it and realise that it had all been a bad dream (and that I was not hurting inside anymore). My thoughts were so close to unravelling my mind completely, as you can only tug at a thread for so long before the whole thing comes apart.

I feared for my already narrow scope of reality… to put it mildly. I sat fearful and hunched. I momentarily closed my eyes and pressed my fingers to my lids, cutting off the impending tears as I was having trouble keeping it all together. I just hoped that it did not appear as an admittance of guilt...

My thought pattern was suddenly interrupted as Detective Sergeant Armstrong reached into a large manila envelope and four colour photos were placed horizontally across the desk in front of me.

"Do you recognise any of these women?" It was Detective Constable Regan who had spoken.

I eyed the photographs with a mixture of sickened interest and heartbreak, my body going cold at the thought and teeth becoming on edge.

After studying the photographs for a despairing few moments I had immediately recognised them as being of the four women who had recently been murdered. Their photographs had been splashed all over the television and newspapers for weeks on end, so I could hardly have failed to recognise them.

I closed my eyes briefly and set the photographs aside.

I fought back the urge to ask them if I could take a 50/50, ask the audience or phone a friend. I figured, wisely, that it would make me even less popular with the officers… and I would hate to take an accidental tumble next time I went down any stairs here.

Underneath the table my hands clenched and unclenched tensely at the thought of the confrontation that I was now somewhat reluctantly engaged in. I glanced up, trying to keep my dignity intact as I answered.

"Well, yes. They look like the murdered women whose pictures have been all over the media of late, and obviously I knew Nikki Chandler personally."

I pointed to the picture next to Nikki. It showed a young auburn haired woman with a complexion as clear as fine china.

"This one I recognise from her working at my local supermarket, although I did not know her personally."

Detective Sergeant Armstrong fixed me with his gaze, a baleful stare. His tone was inculpatory with every question sounding like an accusation.

"So you have never met these other two women?"

I gave a slow shake of my head. I was too exhausted to be angry but still remained filled with vague panic. I felt awkward and inadequate and I squirmed uneasily in my chair, as I responded.

"No, not to my knowledge."

"So you would not be able to tell us how your mobile number got into one of their address books?"

Detective Sergeant Armstrong let the question hang in the air.

Momentarily speechless, I frowned my puzzlement before attempting to reply.

"Nnn... no," I stammered.

My head was swirling and I could barely speak. I was in total shock and could offer no more words, so I sat dumfounded in the midst of the barrage of further questions being aimed at me. For those despairing few minutes, I was filled with boundless anxiety and trepidation and felt my eyes fill with tears. How I silently cursed the police officers and what they had done to me. I shivered involuntarily and hugged myself tightly as this was not the most comfortable environment I had witnessed and I was feeling somewhat chilled.

Meanwhile, the officers watched me intently, as if they were hawks homing in on a rodent. Their gaze was unblinking with undisguised hate and I could sense that they thought they were close to unravelling my story. They were obviously currently revelling in my confused and frightened persona. Our gazes locked for a moment as we just sat and stared at one another.

I was clearly frustrated and desperately struggling for control, whilst their distain was making me feel small and naked. This only fed my own rage as I knew that they were waiting to leap at on any mistake I made and any sign of weakness on my part.

It seemed as inevitable as the grave.

Diane's gaze fastened on my now ashen face as she laid a conciliatory hand on my arm. I felt myself flinch a little at the contact, before examining my memory to answer the officers' question.

"I could not tell you how my mobile number got into their address book. I really do not know. Perhaps we shared a common friend? Perhaps I dealt with her in a professional capacity when I was in the investment game. I may have been recommended to her by an acquaintance, or I could have even bought or sold something from or to her in the past... there are a dozen possible ways..."

I realised this sounded lame even as the words left my mouth. The sentence was left unfinished as my words trailed off, but hung in the air for what seemed an endless moment. Even as I had spoken the words, I heard my own doubt creep in. I met the officers' glares with an unblinking stare, hoping that they would sense that I was genuine.

I was to be disappointed.

My attempted explanation obviously did not prove to be a satisfactory answer as the question was repeated, before I was then probed for what seemed like hours over my movements and whereabouts on a variety of given dates. Their questions rained down upon me in staccato fashion, but not being a walking filofax I struggled to verify my exact whereabouts, so I could give no concrete alibi on any of the dates that the officers were concerned with. I could give no exact statement of fact as the details were still hazy in my mind. Snatches of conversation and images flew past, but were meaningless and seemed out of context.

I had left my previous employment a couple of months ago and prior to that I had been off work, with stress related illness, for an additional four months. So for the last six months I had rarely ventured out from the sanctuary of my apartment, aside from the retail therapy of the odd shopping expedition or my counselling sessions with Samantha or my excursions to paint...all of which, like masturbation, I kept as solo pursuits.

As I lived alone I obviously had no-one to verify my whereabouts. I had almost become a recluse as a result of my marriage breakdown and then subsequently being shunned by my friends. I took refuge in a bottle...well hundreds actually and had also become hooked on prescription drugs. I had an addictive personality...

Exhaustion had worn down my defences, I was not doing well.

My eyes filled with quiet grief as the interview was turning out exactly as I had been expecting and dreading.

I felt cold with fear and frustrated rage, so I longed for secluded tranquillity. I wished now, that I had taken up the option of the previously prepared statement and declined any further questioning, as it would have calmed the confusion currently crashing about inside my head.

I wondered if it were now too late to take that option?

"Do you recall being outside Miss Chandler's house at approximately 6pm on the evening of the 8th August? That was the evening that she was last seen alive. A neighbour of hers has stated that a man matching your description was seen hanging about in the street outside Miss Chandler's house for about an hour. Does this ring any bells with you?"

He spoke as if he were enticing a moth to a flame. He thought I was trapped and was determined to take full advantage of the fact. As he leaned towards me his eyes bored into mine, intent on an answer. His tone had gone hard and his words pounded as he leaned closer to me. I watched his shoulders tense then relax. I felt as if I were a rabbit trapped in the headlights of an oncoming vehicle. His expression made me momentarily falter, but despite the continuing pressure and intimidation almost snapping the last restraint on my temper, I still managed a reply.

"No. Not that I recollect."

I could hear the desperation in my voice, as if I subconsciously had resigned myself to an inevitable fate. It was not an act (as the officers were surmising) as I genuinely could not remember much about that evening. I remembered leaving the Portobello Road market and planning to walk back via Nikki's house but I could not recall if I actually had or not as the journey that I eventually took home was pretty much a complete blank to me, (although I did recall telephoning Nikki very late that same evening but only reaching her answering machine). My previous emotional scarring and my current attachment to Prozac and brandy chasers were obviously not conducive to me sustaining any real clarity of thought or memory.

I knew how this was making me sound and that things looked bad for me at the moment (and would probably get a damned sight worse). I drifted into familiar reverie. My thoughts danced through my mind as I realised that nothing in my life made sense any more. I felt my shoulders drop and my body slouch forward as mentally I retreated deeper and deeper into the maze of myself. I shivered, then straightened, but still refusing or unable to conform I answered again with exaggerated patience and felt my throat tighten as I spoke.

"I really do not know. I can not remember going back to Nikki's but I may have done as I purchased a bracelet which I was going to give her if she was in, but I do not recall if I went home via her house or not. I still had the bracelet with me the next morning so I would assume that I did not. I do remember telephoning her much later that evening but I only reached her answer-phone service. I left a message...you can check her tape and my itemised phone bill, if you do not believe me.

I suffer from blackouts sometimes and have done on and off for the last twenty years. I have no control over them.

"You can check with my doctor and my psychiatrist...IF you have not already. All I can do is try to tell you the truth as I am remembering it."

I felt my body shudder again as it stiffened. I just hoped that the officers would believe my obvious sincerity but alas not. I was informed that an identification parade would be arranged if I continued to deny my presence at the crime scene at the time stated. I felt wearied by the way the conversation was progressing and I felt like I wanted to cry but I was all cried out.

I sensed that the detectives just felt that I was disturbing and was trying to hoodwink them. Nothing could be further from the truth. Well, perhaps I was just a little disturbing...

I let the thought drift.

My gaze shot up again as I could sense them analysing my every word and scrutinizing my body language as they snorted impatiently. I shifted uneasily in my seat, too flustered now to concentrate. How I loathed it and the way it set my teeth on edge. I imagined how pleasant it would be to live in a world free of pain and suffering. Even as the notion flitted through my mind, I jolted back to my own dire situation.

The officers seemed convinced that the evidence and what I was saying were two different things entirely.

I had been sitting there for hours doing my best to answer their inane questions over and over again, whilst the Keystone Cops bellowed in front of me. Several times the duty solicitor had to intervene when the detectives had deliberately said something hurtful to get a rise out of me and to catch the pain in my expression. Their actions made me quail as they toyed with me as a cat would with a mouse.

I had been verbally attacked, castigated, vilified and railed against...and so far I had only been there for a morning!

I suspected that for my remaining time there, each minute would seem like an eternity.

I could not stand it as I did not enjoy being scrutinized as if I were some laboratory rat. I just hoped that I was not remembering inaccurately. The thought made me feel uncomfortable but I could not dislodge it from my brain.

We spent the next minute or so frozen in silence, fixing each other with stares. For a split second I caught a glimpse of cruelty in their eyes that sent a shiver down my spine. I was once again a frightened child, as all the thin veneer of adult self-confidence seemed to have been peeled away by these officers.

Thankfully a break in the proceedings was called in order that we all could get some food and refreshments. I did not disagree to the suggestion or offer another word, as I felt all talked out.

The interview was terminated and the tapes were stopped whereupon the two officers arose and vacated the room leaving the duty solicitor and I alone. I got up from the chair and began to pace, eager to stretch my legs. I reached for the pack of cigarettes on the table and lit one, inhaling deeply, stifling a sigh of relief... God I needed that.

Diane looked up and gave me a small restricted smile. Her gaze fastened on my pale face as she took my hand, probably to stop it shaking. I felt myself trembling against her skin as her voice, soothing and reassuring, floated over me.

"You are doing fine. Just adhere to your version of events and just try to relax and do not let them get under your skin. I realise that it is not easy but I am sure that they will soon realise their mistake and release you. The evidence that they have produced thus far is purely circumstantial and there has been no forensic evidence produced as yet. Motive and state of mind will have to be established, and at present, the officer's seem to be clutching at straws. You have to understand that there is a lot of pressure on the police to secure a result and in their eyes, with your prior record and association to at least one of the victims; you are viewed as the ideal fall guy. I feel sure that they will soon realise that the Crown Prosecution Service will not progress with the case as it stands. Obviously the officers have now called a break, so they will be rechecking your statements, examining the property and effects taken from your apartment earlier this morning and probably contacting your doctor and analyst, now that you have given your consent for them to do so. It will all get straightened out, given time and I am sure that everything will eventually be fine for you."

I studied her face for any sign of dissembling but saw none, but still I gave a non-committal grunt (whilst trying to stifle a yawn).

God, I felt tired. I just hoped that Diane was correct and that this was just a temporary stay (and the more temporary the better) as at present the worries were gnawing through my gut.

Just then there was an abrupt knock on the door and two uniformed police officers, one carrying a clipboard, entered the room. I was informed that I was to be escorted to a holding cell whilst further enquiries were to be made. To my ears, it sounded feeble. It sounded a desperate pretext. Surely the truth was that they wanted to keep me on tenterhooks for a while longer, to grind me down and rattle my nerves.

Hesitating, I turned as I reached the door, looking back at Diane for reassurance. She smiled and mouthed:

"You will be OK."

Our eyes met. I felt mine well up and quickly rubbed my hand over them. I had a strong feeling and it was an unpleasant one as my voice sank barely above a whisper.

"Please get me out of here."

"I will do my best," Diane replied, matter-of-factly.

I gave a helpless shrug as I inhaled, but did not reply.

Diane nodded to me, no doubt as an act of reassurance, before returning her attention to the writing pad, that was sitting resting on her knee.

I was feeling overwhelmed by the impossibility of understanding the two interviewing officers and what was making them tick. My head was starting to hurt as my mind struggled to keep up, to piece the fragments together as a million questions ran through my mind.

With Diane's last words ringing in my ears I was escorted along a long winding narrow corridor and down a short flight of stairs, which sent the echoes of our footsteps chasing us. We soon arrived at a row of small cubicles with blackboards situated on the wall outside; upon which were scrawled an abundance of differing names and charges. The officers paused outside the second cell, swung the already ajar door open and ushered me inside. There was more cheer in a cemetery. As I stepped forward, I nearly jumped out of my skin as the metal door was slammed decisively shut behind me. I thought that they could have pre-warned me or even left it open as I was hardly going anywhere.

The sound nagged at my confusion, but I supposed that it was all to be part of the ongoing intimidation process. I heard the squeak of chalk on the small blackboard outside the cell, the sound of which brought goose bumps to my skin and always had done since my long distant school days. It was far from a pleasant sensation. I noted that there was a small gap three quarters of the way up the door, which was just a little bit wider than a letterbox. I walked towards it to peer out but just then two eyes appeared on the other side, whereupon it was forcefully shut on me. I wondered if it were more of a wearisome habit than a necessity, or was just to add to the continuing intimidation process. I retreated to the back of the cell and sat down on the long padded bench. I looked around the bleak confined space. Aside from the bench, a buzzer near the door, and the tangles of dust in the corners the cell was empty. Penned graffiti covered the depressing steel grey walls and it smelt like a toilet. It was a mixture of urine and disinfectant, a distinctly less than fragrant combination. The dim light accumulated on the walls and ceiling and gave the impression that the room was closing in on me. I felt pre-occupied as if lost in a dream.

My watch had been removed earlier so I had no idea what time it now was or exactly how long I had now been in custody. It seemed an eternity but in reality it was probably no more than just a few hours. I bemoaned my plight and wondered if the nation's media, having got wind of an arrest, were now camped resolutely outside the police station. I hoped not, as I was a solitary creature and did not enjoy or trust the vast majority of humans at the best of times (and with good reason). I could just picture my exit from the police station, through a jostling throng that were manhandling me, crowding around and jeering me. Their faces evilly gleeful, relishing my fate. No doubt there would even be parents hoisting their children high up on their shoulders to get a clearer view. I imagined how everyone would delight in my pain and fright. Just how the hell did I get myself into this mess? My thoughts again turned inwardly analysing my woeful existence. If only I could take my mind off the worries that crawled through my brain. God I needed a drink! I did not even have my cigarettes, which still sat upon the interview table or my medication, which I assumed was still in the apartment, to settle my nerves and take the edge off of the acute anxiety and the depression that I was now feeling.

I wondered if my Prozac tablets had been removed from my apartment or whether they were still sitting in my bathroom cabinet. There was no knowing what the police had taken or how much of it I would ever get back. I wished now that I had insisted on a written list of all the seized items from my apartment then and there. I assumed that I could now wave goodbye to any cash or jewellery that I had left there as, in my experience, the police tended to be the human equivalent of magpies. During my years of soliciting and random thieving/shoplifting I had lost count of how many times my 'earnings' had gone astray after 'stop and searches' or arrests.

With a low moan, I leant forward burying my face in my hands. I was feeling so desperate and helpless but trying to not lose hope or admit defeat just yet. I so loathed people analysing my fragmented mind and planning strategies to break me down. I felt as though I were being pushed to the very limit. With this entire emotional trauma, it was just like my schooldays, or being married again. With those memories now to the fore, I felt intense rage just bubbling beneath the surface, a simmering emotion that could erupt at any stage against those who had wronged me.

God, I wished that I could call Samantha as I could almost see my guilty thoughts and dark admissions. As tears filled my eyes I regretted now not having I used her as my 'one phone

118

call' when I was first brought in to this less than palatial abode.

You live at the place inside your head, so perhaps the officers were hoping that my alleged guilt would build up until I was eager to betray myself, and then they would pounce...

My train of thought and spiralling depression faltered as I heard the sound of a key in the lock. I took my head out of my hands and looked up. I silently prayed that it was Ms Keane to tell me that I was now free to go and that it had all been a terrible mistake, but I was to have no such luck as a uniformed police officer appeared. He looked barely out of school, full of pimples and hair gel. I thought for a brief moment that Simon Cowell must have put together a boy band equivalent of the village people. He carried in a plastic tray upon which sat an unidentified meal and a cup of a dubiously coloured liquid. He sat the tray down next to me on the bench and turning silently exited.

Obviously he was not a great one for small talk, and I certainly would not be leaving him a gratuity.

I lifted the cup to my mouth and discovered that the dishwater coloured liquid was in fact tea, although whether the teabag had actually entered the plastic cup or had just been wafted over the top of it was still open to some debate. I placed the cup back down on the tray and lifted the plastic plate to my lap. God, I felt ravenous.

A plastic knife and fork were wrapped in a white serviette, so I pulled them out. I thought that I may have been able to identify the meal once it was nearer to me, but alas not. Against my better judgement I braved a mouthful. I would not be making that terrible mistake again. At least I had finally found something that made airline meals seem edible. I assumed that the police canteen staff was auditioning for a new television series: 'Can't cook, can't be fucked to learn.'

I set the plate back down on the tray and went back to the cup of tea-like substance. It was ghastly but I was parched, so I drank it anyway. Obviously I was still sorely dehydrated from the several bottles of red wine I had consumed last night and early this morning.

Never again!

As I set the cup back on the tray the peephole in the door

clicked open and a pair of eyes leered in. I felt like an exhibit at some outdated freak show or at the local zoo. I resisted the urge to flick food in that direction. I would save that particular game for later in case I got bored.

The door opened and the police officer entered. It was the same pop idol wannabe from previously.

I inhaled deeply as I focussed my attention on him.

"Ah great, room service."

My attempt at sarcasm went un-rewarded as the boy band reject with a complexion of a pepperoni pizza remained silent and paid me no heed. He walked over towards me and picked up the tray, imparting a sneer as he did so. He stared down in disgust at the almost full plate, so obviously I was going to be in trouble for not eating my greens and I felt sure that I would be getting no dessert now.

"Compliments to the chef," I called after him, as he whirled and stalked out, whilst ensuring that the cell door was once again slammed decisively shut behind him.

No sense of humour these young constables. You would have thought that as they had to wear what looks like a tit on their head when they went out on the beat that they would need to have a sense of humour as a necessary job requirement.

Oh well, you live and learn.

I laughed inwardly at my own joke, silently congratulating myself on retaining my sense of humour in such adversity, but now that the show of fake bravado was out of the way I once again slumped forward. The cell was making me feel claustrophobic, and the light seemed dim, as if overpowered by the cell's bleakness. I was conscious of my blood coursing through my veins, of the heat in my head and the roar in my ears. My skin was tingling and my saliva had dried in my mouth as my throat closed up on me. I could feel my heart thumping in my chest, so loud and fast that I feared it may rupture. My head was also spinning like a top as I had so much mentally to digest. My mind had gone numb, frozen and recoiled, unable or refusing to accept or cope with the unfurling events. I seemed unable to lock up my feelings, as my body became light, floating and uncontrolled. I knew that current events were rapidly spiralling out of my control again and that this time the results could be disastrous for me, but I had no solution as to a way to reel them in. I hummed inwardly trying to ease the tension I felt and attempting to keep my mounting anger and bitterness in check.

I was so alone.

I felt tense and restless, like a caged lion, as I paced the floor of the tiny windowless cell, straining to relax. I was still unaware of the time or how long I had now been shut in here. It felt as if I were in a fridge as cold draughts swept through the gaps in the door and teased my skin. I closed my eyes and shivered.

I just had too many thoughts swirling in my head to allow me to settle just yet. Foreboding washed over me as fear caressed me, making me feel strange and intimidated.

I still felt intoxicated from the wine, whilst the interviewing officers seemed drunk with power. It was not a great combination for a stress free day. I wondered what the assessments and feedback from my doctor and Samantha would be.

I hated being trapped and enclosed in such a small space with no windows and stale air, which brought back unwanted memories of the bunker. The gang's images and recollections of that long night came flooding back to me. I recoiled at the mental images of my past horror as I now recognised certain similarities between the two events. Just being trapped here had set my teeth on edge and now the endless waiting was only adding to my ever-expanding sense of unease, my shortness of temper and irritability ever increasing. A procession of flashbacks walked before my eyes, shadowy shapes accusing me and teasing me. I felt sudden rage and slammed my hand hard against the wall, jarring my body. I winced as pain shot up my arm but thankfully the thought process I was previously engaged in had now ceased. I returned to the padded bench and lay out on it, hands behind my head cupping it. I stared up at the ceiling.

God I was bored, and the feeling of isolation overwhelming.

You would have thought that they could have stuck a Pac-Man or Space Invaders machine in here... or a television, just something to pass the time and to alleviate this mental torture.

In a bid to stop me ruminating and pondering my plight further I started reading the graffiti on the walls but most of it was just inane scrawl with just the odd funny quip standing out like a rose amongst the thorns. It struck me how many dyslexic prisoners must have passed through this cell as most comments were inaccurately spelt and some had apparently even struggled to spell their own name correctly.

Oh, the wonders of the modern comprehensives.

Just as I was inwardly bemoaning the country's spiralling education standards I was roused from thought by the sound of the peephole cover being snapped open. I felt like one of those 'models' from the Soho peepshows and I wondered whether I was expected to whip my top off. I did not enjoy being observed like some caged animal so I glared over at the pair of eyes that leered in at me. This action was swiftly followed by the sound of a key in the lock as the heavy metal door sprang open. The two officers that had led me here now stood in the doorway and motioned to me to get up. I did as I was instructed.

One of the officers entered the cell and grabbed my arm to escort me out, which I thought was strange behaviour as I was in a 6ft x 6ft box so hardly could have failed to find my own way out. Perhaps they were judging me by their own high standards?

I was taken back to the interview room the way I had come, so my request to be led back the scenic route was being sadly denied me.

Upon the interview room door being swung open I saw Ms Keane seated poring over the documents that were spread out on the table in front of her, her nose scrunched up in concentration. A plastic cup of what looked like black coffee sat a fair distance from her on the table, obviously to avoid any spillage on the aforementioned documents. She looked up as I entered and acknowledged my presence with a brief but warm smile.

The officers wavered before slowly turning to depart the interview room, causing me to have visions of them holding out their hands for a gratuity as they did so.

They remained outside the door, which had I noted been left very slightly ajar (so I knew that I would have to be careful what I said). As I scanned the room, it was Diane who was first to speak.

"How are you feeling now?"

I initially struggled for composure and for something to say, as trying to kill the pain I swore silently under my breath.

"OK, I suppose. I still feel slightly tired and hung-over thanks to being awoken at the crack of dawn. I do not even remember requesting an early morning wake up call."

"Did they bring you something to eat and drink?"

"After a fashion," I replied bitterly.

I did not explain the statement, although in truth my stomach was probably too knotted to get a bite of food down anyhow.

Diane opened her mouth as if to speak but then closed it again, obviously deciding that she did not want to go there.

Goldfish impressions over, she once again glanced down at the paperwork that was spread out thinly before her.

I took the seat next to her as I lit a, by now much needed, cigarette. The nicotine rush was almost instant and I could feel my body immediately crying a 'thank you' as I inhaled hungrily.

When I finally broke free of my nicotine trance, I turned to Diane.

"Have there been any new developments?"

"Not that I have heard but the two interviewing officers should be due back soon. Detective Sergeant Armstrong popped his head round the door about five or ten minutes ago and said that they were going to grab a sandwich, and would only be a quarter of an hour or so. "

If they were from the police canteen it would be a damned sight quicker than that, I mused. A full minute of silence followed, I tried to raise a smile but my lips faltered and fell into a tired line.

I was just in the process of stubbing out my cigarette into the solitary ashtray sitting upon the large oak table, when the interview room door opened and Detective Sergeant Armstrong and Detective Constable Regan re-entered the room. They pulled out the chairs opposite Ms Keane and me, and sat down, whilst placing files and manila envelopes on the desk in front of them. Detective Constable Regan nodded an acknowledgement to us whereupon he reached over and depressed the record button on the tape recorder. As the machine clicked to life and emitted a faint hum he proceeded to inform the machine that the interview had commenced, announced the time and the persons present.

Had I not been here before?

I was not sure why but as he spoke I felt myself breaking out in beads of icy perspiration, the tension thrumming through me as my body turned cold. God, I desperately needed some sleep.

I mentally tried to ward off the growing chill as once again an intense sense of foreboding crept over me. My memories of Nikki that lingered were all warm and erotic but the details were becoming fuzzy now. I felt an awful sadness and a great sense of loss as I desperately tried to fight back the tears of pain that had sprung to my eyes at my minds recollection of her. I was unable to hold back the emotion and my vision had now become blurred by tears.

Diane handed me a tissue and placed her hand on my arm in a compassionate and consoling gesture as if she had read my thoughts.

"Are you OK, or would you like the interview paused?"

I sighed, not at my memories, nor even my loss, but at this obvious misunderstanding. I felt the words jam in my throat, desperate for release.

"No... I will be OK. Sorry. I was thinking about Nikki.

It just all got to me."

A flash of rage had burst within me but I noted that my voice had fallen to a barely audible quivering whisper as I tried to forestall any further embarrassment.

I swallowed and tried again to orate but although I could feel my tongue working, I could no longer speak.

Inside my rage grew steadily hotter as mentally I felt as if I had been buffeted by a gale. I studied the officers' angry faces as the questions were once again fired at me at a machine gun rate.

Frustration manoeuvred into my brain as I was becoming increasingly annoyed and agitated by this type of interrogation. The officers were obviously tainted by the same suspicious nature that I had as their gaze was burning in its intensity and had led to a crawling sensation moving eerily across my skin.

As the interview droned on in the same antagonistic and repetitive manner as before the break in proceedings, I felt that

124

any spark of hope that had long since glimmered had now been fully extinguished. The officers were just not accepting or, more importantly, believing a single word I was saying, no matter what form of response I tried. They automatically assumed that I had convenient amnesia, but memories grow dim, so there seemed no prospect of finding the answers to placate them. They had no right to treat me in this way. No right to demand different answers to the same questions, over and over again...

I felt confused and avoided the officers' eyes as I did not want to see the disbelief I knew would be there. I'd had enough as the cross-examination had become utterly farcical and the officers' attitudes were ranging from contempt to barely concealed hostility. I refused to rise to the bait, so I dug my heels in and was determined to not give them any more of my assistance. I could not even imagine dignifying such questions with an answer as my mind clamped shut.

Diane's gaze fastened on my rapidly perspiring face as question after question received a 'no comment' response.

I was informed by the officers that, 'I was not helping myself'.

SILENCE

When I did not speak, I was informed that I did not have the right to silence (so much for supposedly living in a democracy).

I was angry and disappointed and as I glowered at the officers, I could feel myself rapidly losing control of the situation.

Now I was stressed.

"NO COMMENT THEN!"

Both the officers' expressions, tone and voices were now openly becoming more hostile towards me. The sniping had begun, whilst their manner was despotic and oppressive. Their eyes blazed hate, they seemed to be under the impression that their relentless badgering and intimidation (in conjunction with no edible food or sleep) would somehow lead me to break down and that I would throw myself down in front of them whilst confessing my sins. I could not help but think that their strategy and approach seemed more akin to the Witch Finder General and prisoner of war camps, than to modern day policing, but what the hell did I know?

I had a feeling that this would turn out to be longest day ever as I already felt totally fatigued and doubted that it was even midday yet.

After a while I turned away to count the bricks in the wall as the dialogue that assaulted my ears was far from enthralling. Even the pretty pictures that I had to look at earlier had ceased to be there. It was times like this that I wished that I had brought my travel solitaire or at least a deck of cards. I resisted the urge to ask the officers if they wished to participate in a game of 'scissors, paper, and stone'.

Still the questions continued with unerring regularity despite me now not even facing the officers and still continuing to give non committal 'no comment' responses or, more often then not, just complete silence. The atmosphere had become cloying and oppressive as the officers continually tried to rile me and to get under my skin. At one point I opened my mouth to say something but then thought better of it, closing my mouth with a sharp snap. I could not find the words as my chest and throat were too locked in a combination of rage and sadness to speak, my throat raw. Anxiety surged again, shoving all rational thoughts from my brain. Inwardly I snarled with fury but outwardly I remained silent, refusing to even acknowledge their intimidating presence. That would seem like admitting defeat somehow and I could not have them breaking through my guard.

A cold shiver ran through me, as there was an odd incomplete moment when none of us spoke. I think perhaps all of us now realising the futility of what was now taking place. The silence was only parted by the sound of our own heavy breathing.

With the officers booming monotonous voices and all the relentless badgering I was getting a crucifying migraine.

I noted the officer's anger and frustration as it flashed across their faces. Their mouths were stiff, blood flaring high on their cheeks. My optimism was also fading fast and despondency now had lodged in my gut, as I failed to see the point of all their red-faced manipulation. Thankfully as the officers were getting nowhere the interview was then abruptly curtailed and the tapes stopped. Detective Sergeant Armstrong and Detective Constable Regan both arose and with their eyes burning and scowls hardening, stormed angrily out of the interrogation room, slamming the door behind them. The door was left rattling in its frame and its hinges vibrating as Ms Keane and I sat alone.

I assumed they thought that she would try to dissuade me from my continued course of action and negotiate a compromise, although I personally did not have any qualms about my silence.

I was finding speaking reasonably increasingly difficult and I knew that I had to proceed with caution.

As a low murmur of conversation fluttered from the corridor outside into the room, I arose and began to pace, as sitting there for hours had been making my back ache and my joints feel stiff. I reached for another cigarette and upon lighting it blew clouds of smoke up towards the ceiling, temporarily masking the horrendous strip lighting above me.

Diane was the first to speak as she looked at me quizzically.

"You were telling me the truth weren't you?"

My eyes narrowed as I met her stare with one of my own.

"Yes, of course I was. Great, so you do not believe me now either?" I said accusingly, my voice now edged more with anger than frustration. I felt trapped deep within myself with no way out, not even words.

As I loomed over her, Diane tried to keep her voice gentle and her tone light, but I could hear the tightness creeping in as she spoke.

"Jamie, I do believe you, but you need to convince the officers. If you do not waver from your story, no matter how many times the officers ask you, eventually they will have no choice but to believe you or at least doubt their initial suspicions. I realise that you are under no obligation to answer any questions but you are not really helping yourself to clear this matter up. If you continue with your 'no comment' responses they will look at it as if you are reaffirming your guilt to them, plus now-a-days a jury can draw adverse inference from the accused relying on evidence not mentioned to the police at the time of the arrest and subsequent questioning."

Although this appeared to vanquish all reason, I muttered

an apology of sorts before continuing (the loss of my temper was just enough to give my voice an edge).

"But how can the officers absolve me when they are not taking in a single word I say or believing any viable explanation I give?

I feel as if I am banging my head against a brick wall."

All that I was feeling previously was cold resentment towards the officers but (now with the situation that I have since found myself in) it was turning into pure hatred and contempt.

I felt my chest rise and fall in a long silent sigh.

"You must remain positive. As the old saying goes, do not let the bastards grind you down."

I inhaled slowly, deeply, before I managed a small smile and responded.

"I will try not to."

Diane rubbed a hand over her mouth and bit down on her lower lip thoughtfully before speaking.

"Right, then stay focused, if you do not impede their investigation, perhaps you will satisfy their curiosity faster. It looks like they have gone to lick their wounds and probably make some further enquiries. They will probably make you wait back in the holding area in an attempt to soften you up, so is there anything you need to ask me before you go?"

As I replied, I felt myself becoming light-headed with juggling too many emotions all at once.

"No. Not really. I am innocent… but I just can't prove it yet, so you will just have to take my word for it."

Diane looked me in the eyes as she lowered her voice.

"I do believe you and be assured that I will do everything within my power to get you out of here."

I gave a slight smile, before responding.

"Thank you, it is appreciated, and my apologies for earlier but I was just getting so frustrated with them and their snide innuendos. This whole thing just does not make any sense to me."

"I understand, you were angry and with good reason, but you do not want to widen the rift between yourself and the officers as it will only make things worse for you."

I silently wished that the evidence did not seem quite so

incriminating…

Just then the interview room door swung open and the two uniformed officers from previously stood oppressively framed in the doorway.

"You are to be escorted back to the holding cell whilst ongoing enquiries are made, so if you would like to come with us…"

I assumed that they were addressing me unless Ms Keane was now under suspicion for the kidnapping of Shergar or some other unsolved crime from the mists of time.

"Not really, but I suppose that I have no choice?"

They gave me a dismissive twist of the lips (as they eyed me standing there) before speaking coldly.

"No, now get up."

I felt angry and bewildered as if I had been rudely awakened.

I was now back where I started all those years ago, desperate, needy and alone, with despair eating away at my very fibre. Recall sent a cold shiver through me and I took a deep breath. I could barely contain my impatience as I rose lethargically from my chair and walked towards the officers who grabbed my arms and led me away, much to my chagrin. I assumed that when they said that 'ongoing enquiries were being made', that it really meant that the officers had sidled off with their tails between their legs to lick their wounds whilst planning the next course of action, intimidation and hostility. As neither officer appeared to have the capacity for free thought I surmised that I could be left cooped up in that tiny cramped space for a fair while yet. I sensed that they were preparing tensely for something to be aimed at me. At this thought, the serpent of rage ran through me but I tried to swallow back the feeling.

I certainly would not be coming back to this guesthouse again, that was for damned sure...

I was led back to the same cell that I had occupied previously and I noted that my name and the charges I now faced were chalked up on the small blackboard outside.

Both had even been spelt correctly, wonders would never cease.

The taller of the two officers leant forward to swing open

the door. As I entered I felt a stab of intense pain shoot through my body from my kidneys. The punch had snatched my breath away, making me weave unsteadily, eventually toppling towards the wall. As I stumbled, I instinctively flung my arms out in front of me as I fell forward...

With a flutter my eyes opened as doubled over and gasping I drifted back to semi-consciousness. I felt myself being gripped by the arms and lifted but my legs buckled repeatedly. I felt dazed and groggy as shock ran through me and I could feel myself swaying feebly. For a few moments I could not remember where I was or what had happened. When I had regained some of my senses and was back on my feet, albeit unsteadily, I could feel a trickle of blood running down the side of my face. I inhaled sharply as my mouth opened and closed, struggling for breath. I felt an intense pain in my kidneys and then it all came flooding back to me... the rabbit punch. I wondered which of the spineless bastards the aggressor was. They did not even have the guts to confront me face to face; they had to sucker punch me. I straightened up. My head was pounding but I tried to ignore the pain although I could hear the sound of the blood pumping in my ears. My eyes went hard as rage simmered behind them.

Just then the custody sergeant, alerted no doubt by all the commotion, appeared in the doorway of the cell.

His anger was not directed at me.

"What the bloody hell has happened here?!" he bellowed.

It was the taller officer who responded.

"The prisoner fainted whilst we were putting him back in the cell. He fell forward before we had the opportunity to catch him and he hit his head on the wall there."

He actually pointed, even though there was a thin trail of blood gleaming from the pale painted brickwork. Surely the custody sergeant, although probably no Sherlock Holmes, could have worked it out?

If I were not in so much pain I would have laughed. Instead I briefly closed my eyes.

Undaunted by the fact that his story had more holes in it than a fishing net, the officer continued to accentuate...

"The prisoner left his lunch and reeks of booze, so perhaps

it is no wonder that he is a bit light headed?"

I was sure that he sneered.

The custody sergeant nodded cautiously, seemingly unwilling to believe the evidence first-hand. He visibly tensed as he looked across at me for confirmation of this fable, but when I just looked to the floor he verbalised the question.

"Is that true?"

My voice wavered as I replied.

"What, that I feel 'light-headed'? Well I do now."

"You know what I meant. Did the incident happen as this officer has stated?"

I smiled grimly as I wiped my brow and a sigh rippled through me.

"I think you already know the answer to that, it is par for the course isn't it?"

My rueful smile had turned into a snarl but as I was still feeling quite winded my voice was barely audible. The sergeant's gaze shunted towards me again, brows knitted and tone changed.

"If you wish to make a formal complaint against either of these two officers I will arrange for a formal statement to be taken from you, and I can assure you that the matter will be fully and meticulously looked into. I will get the doctor down here to check you over, take a look at that cut and to ensure that you are not suffering from mild concussion. How do you feel?"

My eyes were in danger of glazing over and I was too busy trying to fight my pounding headache to think clearly. I attempted to keep calm although my thoughts were sour.

"Just peachy," I murmured blurrily.

Although I knew that it was not the custody sergeant's fault, I had to blame someone for the physical and emotional torment that I had been undergoing.

He enunciated slowly whilst studying me intensely.

"Do you wish to make a complaint?"

I glared as I responded and could no longer hide my exasperation.

"As if there is any point…Just forget it. I will see the doctor though as I have a blinding headache and I have had none of my antidepressants for over twenty-four hours now, and believe me in this place I need them!"

He returned my look without expression.

The two uniformed officers had sidled off, like the cockroaches they were, so just the custody sergeant and I remained in the cell. There had been no apology, only a lingering look before they left. It was a warning I fully intended on heeding.

I braced myself for another aural or physical assault but it did not come, instead the custody sergeant just opened his mouth to speak softly. I saw his momentary frown and a glimmer of regret in his eyes. I sensed that he was plainly embarrassed and disturbed by what had just happened.

"OK, it's your decision, but if you reconsider you can speak to an officer from a special complaints and discipline department of the police service. They will record your complaint and then investigate under the supervision of one of the members of the independent police complaints authority. You can have your solicitor present with you. Just think it over."

His voice was becoming almost paternal as he continued.

"I will send the doctor down straightaway as you have got a small cut and what looks like a nasty bump coming up on your forehead. You may need to put some ice on in to get the swelling down."

He looked earnest and hopeful (and I did not want to tar them all with the same brush as I sensed that he was a good and fair man) but I still grunted a non-committal response.

The sergeant promptly turned and exited the cell, clicking the door behind him. The peephole was left open and I noted a pair of eyes peering through, presumably to ensure that I did not pass out again before the doctor had arrived (or more likely to ensure that I did not inflict any self-imposed injuries before then deciding to log a formal complaint for police brutality). Both the officers and I knew that now we had adopted America's claim culture that there were more than enough ambulance chasing solicitors out there who would willingly take on such a case and revel in the subsequent publicity that came with it.

I still felt slightly winded and groggy and my sight was still slightly hazy. I tried to take deep breaths but my breath was still too laboured. I could feel my heart pounding from the adrenaline rush and I noted the goose pimples on my skin… damn this cell was cold. My head started pounding again as blood thundered in my ears. God I needed an aspirin… and a bodyguard.

My mind drifted for just a brief moment as even thinking was painful. It had been almost fourteen years since my last visit to such an esteemed establishment and unfortunately the welcome and hospitality were as warm and heartfelt as ever…

I breathed hard to contain my mounting anger.

Just then I heard the jangle of keys and the lock of the cell door clicked open. There stood Diane, the custody sergeant and another man with short neatly parted grey hair and greying eyebrows that met in the middle like a pair of mating caterpillars. His eyes were dark and calm, almost dreamy, but watchful. He was soberly attired in a dated dark brown pinstripe suit, white shirt and a chocolate brown tie. As he was clutching a black leather physicians bag (the likes of which I had not seen since the Jack the Ripper movies), I obviously took it as read that he was the police doctor. Nevertheless, he was formally introduced to me, before he prepared to set about checking my sight, head and lungs… as I was still having trouble with my breathing.

He ventured towards me, knelt down and pulled open the aforementioned bag, from which (as a ripple of trepidation ran through my body) he withdrew a pair of latex gloves. Fortunately I did not need to bend over and touch my toes as he just proceeded to examine my head wound. He cleaned the wound with some kind of antiseptic that stung like hell and a swab type thing (that looked like a giant's cotton bud) was applied and held with steady pressure for a good few minutes. I assumed that the bleeding had then ceased as I could no longer feel the blood tricking down my forehead and the doctor applied a large sticking plaster. He then proceeded to press lightly on the lump that had come up on my head.

"Ouch!"

"Sorry, did that hurt?"

The winner of the most obviously question of the year award goes to…

I touched my forehead gingerly, skating over the lump that had arisen there, before replying.

"Just a tad."

"Sorry. Are you experiencing any dizziness or have you a headache?"

"The latter, I feel like a herd of elephants are currently playing field hockey inside my head."

I had always been a tad prone to exaggeration but it helped break the tension up a wee bit.

Smelling salts were then wafted under my nose as I recoiled.

The doctor informed me that even though a person who had suffered a mild concussion may appear fine within a few minutes it can take up to twenty four hours to regain their normal mental functioning. This news was far from comforting, and it crossed my mind that the officers conducting the case must therefore be in a permanent state of concussion, but I thought better of voicing such a statement as I did not wish to incur another unfortunate 'accident'. I was informed that arrangements would be made to obtain my antidepressants for me, which was a blessing as I was feeling extremely fraught and becoming increasingly stressed out. At least the Prozac would take the edge off of those feelings and keep the mounting depression in check. I was then handed some painkillers and a plastic cup filled with water, from the chilled water dispenser in the corridor outside the cell, with which to wash them down.

After I had swallowed the tablets the doctor set about examining my pupils although I was not quite sure what he was checking for. I assumed that the pupils must either dilate or reduce in size if a patient was suffering from concussion but I was not sure which, and I was not really interested enough to bother to enquire.

I was informed that if my headache did not subside or worsened or if I was later experiencing any dizziness, vomiting or memory loss I was to ask to see him immediately.

As regards to the latter…how would I remember what he had just told me? As I did not want to upset him I decided to let the question float unanswered in my mind.

The doctor then turned to the custody sergeant and informed him that I was not to be subjected to any further interrogation for the next twenty-four hours. I was immediately grateful but the custody sergeants face was a picture…a real Kodak moment.

"OK, doctor. I will inform the interviewing officers involved in the case."

I only wished that I could have seen the look on their faces as the news was broken to them. It would have provided a memory to cherish forever. I snapped back to reality as I heard the custody sergeant continuing to orate.

"If you would like to follow me, I will show you out."

The doctor turned and bid me good-day. I thanked him and shaking hands he departed with the custody sergeant, both of them conversing in hushed tones down the corridor. Obviously they were no longer concerned that I would abscond as the cell door was left slightly ajar whilst Diane (who had remained loitering in the doorway throughout) walked across and sat abreast of me. As she crouched over me, like a lioness protecting her cub, her expression seemed to be a mixture of incredulity, anger and concern, a kind of furious sympathy.

As she spoke, she laid her hand on my arm, a comforting gesture.

"How are you feeling really?"

I rubbed the back of my aching neck as shards of pain coursed through my body.

"I am OK, if you discount the jackhammer I have going off in my head at present."

"What happened?"

I felt my face grow hot and anger snarled within me as I answered.

"Oh, did you not hear? I fainted and hit my head on the wall before the gallant officers had the chance to change into their superhero costumes and prevent it."

Her face was flushed with exasperation.

"Mmmm. Now what really happened?"

As my breath caught, I attempted a somewhat evasive reply.

"It does not matter, as I am not pressing charges or making a statement. I have had a bellyful of this place and their bureaucracy as it is without adding to it. I am not the first person to meet with an unfortunate accident whilst in custody and I am damned sure that I will not be the last."

Diane's eyes darkened with rage.

"So they assaulted you? You really do need to report it. The officers responsible cannot be allowed to get away with that behaviour. It is totally unacceptable, barbaric even. You have certain rights; you are entitled to be treated humanely and with respect. Something needs to be done..."

Diane continued to vent her spleen for a good few minutes, and at one point I was deciding whether or not I should go and fetch her a soap box to stand on. Thankfully she stopped short of involving Liberty, Amnesty International and the United Nations peace-keeping force.

I said that I would think over what she had said, but I did not really want to make any decisions right now as I was still feeling a bit groggy and my head was still pounding somewhat.

Diane said that she understood and that she would leave me in peace, to try and rest, whilst she took the opportunity to peruse copies of the case notes and files the interviewing officers had since supplied her with. On rising, she gave me a quick squeeze (I assumed as a sign of reassurance) and stepped back.

I smiled rather wistfully as I thanked her and she departed the cell. I remained seated as the custody sergeant re-emerged and enquired as to whether there was anything that I needed.

I replied that I would not mind a sandwich or a roll as the previous meal had been totally inedible and I had not now eaten for over forty-eight hours.

He looked shocked but replied that it would not be a problem and did I want anything to drink.

I replied that a glass of water would be fine.

He then hastily disappeared, closing the cell door behind him.

Ideally I would not have wanted to risk police canteen food again but I was feeling incredibly light headed, so I felt as though I should try to force something down.

I was becoming restless with my mind shifting uneasily, snatching feebly at passing thoughts, vainly searching for the answers that just would not be forthcoming. I could sense the struggle within me, but the images and memories were too mixed to make sense of them.

Thankfully my train of thought was soon broken, as a few minutes later the custody sergeant reappeared clutching a white plastic tray with what looked like a cheese and ham sandwich wrapped in the mandatory cellophane, a packet of cheese and onion crisps, a plastic beaker of water and thankfully my medication.

God bless him.

The custody sergeant handed the items to me and I thanked him appropriately.

"Is there anything else you need?"

"I couldn't have a pillow, oh, and a blanket could I, as it is freezing in here?"

"Not a problem."

He slipped back out of the door reappearing moments later clutching a grey cotton blanket and a lone pillow, which he handed to me.

They had both seen better days and as I draped the blanket over my shoulders (for comfort as much as warmth), I did not even want to contemplate how many families of dust mites had currently (and previously) made their home in them.

"Thank you."

I felt despite my treatment thus far his actions should be verbally rewarded, so I hid my annoyance under a veneer of good manners. I pulled my legs up and hugged my knees, rocking on my buttocks, as a blaze of pain shot straight through me. God, I hoped the painkillers kicked in soon.

The sergeant turned to go, stopping at the door.

As he turned back to face me, I felt his empathy as he spoke.

"Think over your decision about making the complaint. I do not want thugs on the force as much as you don't… If you have any other problems or if you need anything just press the bell. I will only be at my desk."

I shifted my eyes towards him as my lips twitched. His admission won him bonus points for honesty, so I thanked him and said that I would if required.

As the cell door sprang shut I peeled off the cellophane and bit hungrily into the sandwich. It was a tad stale but still far more edible than my previous offering… and besides I was totally famished.

I felt nauseated by the ravenous hunger and thirst, so I hurriedly pulled open the packet of crisps and laid a few inside the sandwich… just as I had done when I was a child.

As my thoughts regressed I could not help but wonder as to what had become of my parents, my bitch of a wife and the gang's members. History was all I had left and that was filled with bitterness and hurt. I felt so despondent and I wondered if they had received their karma for their actions towards me, or if they had all gone on with their lives totally unaffected.

Knowing my luck, probably the latter.

I wondered if any of them had ever given me a second thought. I thought it unlikely although my parents must have been livid if, or when, their child allowance benefit had been stopped, as they would have had less money to spend down the pub or at the local bookmakers.

I managed a slight smile of satisfaction at that thought but it was not a great act of retribution for the misery they had inflicted upon me, and although I did not feel avenged, it was better than nothing.

After I had reduced the sandwich and the crisps to a ghost of crumbs (and sipped at my water), I lay flat out on the padded bench and plumped up the pillow beneath my head, before curling up foetus-fashion beneath the blanket.

The pain inside my head and my heart were subsiding slightly as I stared out at the bleakly painted battleship grey walls and began counting the bricks. I was feeling very tired as I had slept no more than a few hours in the past week or so. I was becoming drowsy, calm, and remote from the rest of the day's events. I felt my eye lids becoming heavy so I did not try to fight it. The muted throbbing of my brow was subsiding but tears trickled out of my closed eyes. I squeezed them tightly shut and pulling the blanket over me let sleep, as if a fog, descend seductively upon me.

It was a more than long overdue and welcome visitor, though part of me hoped that I would never re-awaken.

CHAPTER 14

DAY 2

I slept more soundly than I had in weeks and upon opening my eyes, it took me a few seconds to realise exactly where I was.

I blinked as the room took focus and my eyes adjusted. Sleep melted away from me as the realization and harsh reality of my location soon came crashing through my dreamlike state. Acute despair and inner torment followed not far behind. I had only just awoken and already I felt utterly miserable, my nerves buzzing as I knew that the day could only get worse and further agonizing days possibly lay ahead for me. I would rather have pretended the situation did not exist as the whole thing was just a joke. I closed my eyes as my mind replayed snatches of yesterday's trauma. I just had to pray that I would be exonerated (and that preferably sooner rather than later), before my whole life went swirling down the gutter. How I longed to hurt those that had hurt me...

I sat up, yawned and stretched, trying to kick start the circulation to my numb and aching limbs (to unlock my muscles sufficiently to be able to stand) whilst my mind attempted to acclimatize to the less than luxurious surrounds that I had awoken within.

The Ritz this was most definitely not.

As I stood up I rubbed the sleep from my eyes and ran my fingers through my tousled mane. There was no mirror in the cell so I was unable to ascertain as to how good or bad I looked, although I certainly felt a lot better and more refreshed after my long and much needed slumber (and my headache thankfully had now subsided considerably). I also felt a lot clearer headed as most of the alcohol, from the previous day, seemed to have now thankfully left my bloodstream, although my mouth still tasted stale and sour. Just then the cell's peephole slid open and a set of unidentified eyes peered in. I hoped that it was not one of my assailants from yesterday (and much to my relief) I discovered that it was not, as the custody sergeant entered the cell and enquired as to how I was feeling. I still felt anxiously defensive and disconcerted (with my mind trying to put a correct interpretation of the actions to date) but I replied that I felt a lot better. He set down a tray beside me, on which sat a paper plate containing a full English breakfast and a polystyrene cup filled with what I assumed to be tea (although after yesterday's experience I was still hedging my bets).

Wow, this was better than how I dined at home.

The sergeant then handed me my medication and a small cup of water.

I thanked him, albeit begrudgingly (as despite his seemingly good intentions he still represented the enemy).

"Have you thought any more about making a statement regarding yesterday's incident?"

I sensed that it was both a question and an apology, but I deliberately kept my expression and response neutral and my response politely non-committal.

"No, not as yet… in truth I have only just woken up. I am sorely tempted to let the whole thing drop, but I will see how today goes first. If I am getting out of here, I would prefer just to put all this fiasco behind me and try to forget that it ever happened."

(In truth I knew that this would never happen, but then perhaps all the truths are lies)?

"Discuss the matter with your solicitor if needs be. Do not be too hasty in making any decision. Think it over."

"OK, I will," I replied, although I knew better than anyone that patience was not one of my greatest virtues.

I was then informed that the doctor would come down to check on me in a short while, after I had eaten, to determine whether or not in his opinion I was up to being questioned further today.

I replied that I was fine.

"The doctor is the one who has to decide that."

The custody sergeant turned and departed, the cell door clanging gently shut behind him.

Silence deadened the room although I sensed that the oppression had lifted somewhat, as it was certainly a bit of a difference from yesterday's slamming and clanking of every available door.

I still felt the discomfort and worry of being here and being wrongly accused, but at present I did not feel the strength of agitation that I had yesterday. Mind you, I had yet to contend with dumb and dumber.

I let my mind wander as memories from the past drifted into my thoughts again, my mental voice reverberating through my head. My own regrets were enough to bury me as they crossed my mind and for a long moment I did not breathe. When I had eventually snapped too, I ate in solitude, tucked hungrily into the breakfast that I had been brought as I was feeling distinctly ravenous. No wonder I was feeling so chilled yesterday, as I'd had no food inside me to act as fuel. My entire intake in the last few days prior to this meal had just been the sandwich and crisps the custody sergeant had graciously brought me last night. No wonder I had felt so under the weather and faint (and obviously the alcohol content had not aided my condition).

I had just devoured the last morsel of breakfast when I heard a key rattling in the lock. I took a final swallow of tea and placing the cup down, set the tray down beside me.

As I looked up, the cell door swung open and in walked the custody sergeant, with the doctor trailing in his footsteps. The latter greeted me warmly and enquired as to how I had slept. I bit back the urge to reply: 'horizontal' and instead replied that I had slept like the proverbial log.

"How have you found your head?"

"It was on my shoulders when I awoke."

The retort had slipped out before I had a chance to stop it.

Obviously was a force of habit.

Humour…or should that be sarcasm, used as a defence mechanism (oh, how my parents and teachers had loathed it).

The doctor, thankfully, had not taken umbrage at the remark and smiled.

Deliberately keeping myself in check, I replied properly this time.

"It seems fine, thank you. I have a dull ache but that may be because I had slept for so long. I had not slept previously for a few days so I was completely washed out. I think exhaustion just

141

finally caught up with me."

I inched upwards from the bench but as I went to arise fully, the doctor took a step forward and asked me to remain seated. He then proceeded to examine my eyes and head.

"They seem fine. You have a bit of a lump that has come up but the cut was not deep and as it did not bleed during the night, it has already begun to scab over. You should be fine."

He opened his bag and reaching inside returned with a couple more painkillers. A glass of water was handed to me and with a couple of gulps the paracetamol were swallowed.

"Are you sure that you are feeling okay. No dizzy spells or nausea during the night or this morning?"

"No, I am fine… thank you."

The doctor turned to the custody sergeant and confirmed that I was fit enough to be interviewed today. The sergeant nodded and stated that the investigating officers would be informed.

I knew that their day would be made.

With that the doctor shut his leather bag and extended his hand with a flourish as he bade me farewell before departing with the custody sergeant. The door closed promptly behind them.

As I sat there staring at the four grim walls I squirmed with discomfort as the thought struck me that I was now about to resume yesterday's hostilities. Was I to dwell on my sins and the inevitable punishment to come?

Perhaps not… surely by now the officers would have had time to check my story, to examine my possessions taken from the apartment and have been able to converse with both my doctor and Samantha. I was sure that they would speak up for me and would not let me down. I sat hunched in anticipation, my stomach cramped in tormented expectation. Hopefully now this whole fiasco would have been straightened out and I would soon be released. I tried to force myself to breath slowly and regularly to calm my anxiety, but that hope was soon crushed as minutes later the custody sergeant re-entered the cell and I was informed that a warrant had been obtained from a magistrate for my continued detention. So I was to spend yet another twenty-four hours in their delightful company. I felt sick, and then furious as their deliberateness felt like thunder. I had expected to be interviewed straight away but I was kept isolated in my cell for what seemed like several hours …obviously in an attempt to 'soften me up', whilst the investigating officers invented new ways in which to pressurise and persecute me. It bewildered me and with nothing to fill the time, my mind began spiralling wildly out of control again. Was it just my imagination troubling me or something that I had suppressed? I felt vaguely disconnected as incoherent flashes of memories and images from the past assaulted my senses. I felt unable to control the thoughts and processes of my mind and I could feel my panic attack worsening as hot surges ran through my body. The horrible nightmares that had tainted my life were now becoming an all too crushing reality and I felt severe dizziness as though I may pass out at any moment. I yearned to prompt my memories, to confirm my recall but I no longer felt able to look into the depths of my heart.

Would this living nightmare never end?!

Just as I was feeling that I may need to take my life to end the pain, a key rattled in the lock and the cell door sprang open. As my heartbeat momentarily faltered, I found myself faced with two uniformed officers who then proceeded to escort me from the cell. After having been permitted to use the toilet and to have a quick wash and a shave, albeit accompanied by the two uniformed police officers, I now found myself within the same soulless interview room as yesterday, with Detective Sergeant Armstrong, Detective Constable Regan and Ms Keane all present. The preliminaries were soon dispensed with once the tape recorder had sparked to life.

It was a different day, but much to my chagrin, it was almost the same questions and tone as the previous one.

How I despaired.

My face flashed with anger, as the frustration set in my eyes.

After yesterday, I had planned to keep my face set hard and emotionless but now I felt in danger of breaking down, so releasing a flood of emotion. I bit down on my lower lip to prevent it from trembling as I felt the emotion begin to well up within me. As the atmosphere noticeably darkened I found that

Diane was proving ineffectual and I began to wonder if she too was beginning to disbelieve my version of events.

The officers' attitudes were definitely getting to me and as the seconds ticked by I could feel the intensity of my feelings beginning to sting and my resolve ending. I felt crushed.

I think my previous personal battles were making this one even more painful for me. My emotions were escalating and I could feel them ricocheting like a pinball machine inside me. I could not endure the discomfort any more and failed to conjure up any positive thoughts, as I felt totally exasperated at having to repeat exactly the same details as I had yesterday, over and over again.

I must have been beginning to sound like a broken record and my expression was sure to have been that of bewilderment if my inner feelings were anything to go by.

To make matters worse for me the police officers' attitude was becoming tiresome and I found myself becoming increasingly exasperated as disbelief set in.

Every time I had to discuss Nikki, I just felt so overwrought and sorrowful, as if I were drowning in an ocean of overwhelming sadness.

As a photograph of Nikki was laid out on the table in front of me I felt the blood drain out of my face and I started to shudder, as if I were having an epileptic fit. I attempted to blink back the tears that had formed.

"Would you like a glass of water?"

It was Diane who had spoken, and she gazed at me like an indulgent teacher as I struggled to get my words out.

"Y-y-yes, thank you."

My annoyance I hoped was suitably hidden under the veneer of politeness.

Detective Sergeant Armstrong arose and with a deep sigh, strode impatiently from the interview room, reappearing a few seconds later with a glass of water, which was then handed to me with a glare, but without a word being spoken.

I tried to keep my tone neutral as I knew that I should not let him know that his prying, threatening and cajoling had needled me (although the tears obviously gave it away).

"Thank you."

I locked his gaze and held it, I could feel him simmering.

I may have grown to hate him but I still remembered my manners, even if I my only reward was a brusque nod.

My hands were trembling wildly so I cupped the container in my hands as I took several unsteady sips of the water. I must have looked as if I were an infant sucking on a dummy for comfort.

I could sense that things were falling apart around me as I swore silently under my breath. I drank some more water but my voice did not really come back, so I sat silent for a moment.

I felt continued discomfort and was becoming increasingly unsettled by the unfurling events as a succession of bagged and tagged exhibits was being rapidly produced before me (as if rabbits being pulled from a top hat). It had been confirmed that traces of my DNA were found on Nikki's body and clothing and in her house, but surely this was to be absolutely no surprise as I had been with her the previous evening (and on the morning of the day that she was tragically stolen from me) but the officers seemed to think that the trace findings were somehow significant, for reasons that I failed to grasp.

Maybe I was just being obtuse?

I set the water down and tried to take a deep calming breath as I felt my agitation rising, before resuming our jerky conversation.

The interviewing officers' demeanour was as curt as ever. I did not have to imagine their impatience in their voices as they were breathing so hard at times that their nostrils turned white.

My head was swimming as I examined my memory. Wave upon wave of questions followed, which went over the same tired old ground time and time again. I barely ungritted my teeth enough to let the replies out. My thoughts were intrusive and upsetting as self-analysis dominated me, and with my anxious worrying I was now agitated beyond belief. My feathers were well and truly ruffled and my patience was now as thin as rice paper. To make matters worse for me all my responses, as ever, dissatisfied the interviewing officers (who appeared robbed of all intelligence) and my solicitor was now turning out to be as much use as a chocolate fireguard. I felt as if I were getting nowhere and being portrayed as a liar. The inner panic felt like a hook in my stomach. All at once the anxiety that I had been suppressing came at me like a tidal wave. When eventually I could take no more of the officers' abasement I sprang to my feet, stiffening my spine as I stretched my neck, pulling myself up to my full height. My face was ever darkening with seething rage and bubbling fury, as I let out a guttural roar…

"Is this some fucking game to you? You are playing Russian Roulette with my life…"

"Sit down… now!"

It was Detective Sergeant Armstrong who had roared back in defiance, his features contorted with rage, as if I had threatened his manhood. He stared at me hard like a Doberman Pincher awaiting the attack command. I could feel the crackle of energy in the air. My eyes were on fire and I could feel myself losing control as I turned to face Diane.

I made sure that the sting of accusation was in my voice as my eyes got harder and my emotions gathered momentum, consumed by the bitterness that I felt.

"Why the hell are you not protecting me? Defending me?"

I felt that I had to shout to get my point across and to exhaust some of my pent-up feelings. Diane looked unbearably apologetic and her cheeks noticeably reddened, but as she opened her mouth to defend herself, she was drowned out by Detective Sergeant Armstrong's booming voice.

"I will not tell you again… take your seat… NOW!"

Blood was crashing through my ears whilst my heart was beating so hard that I thought it may break through my chest completely, but I remained standing as our stares locked, as if two duelling stags, neither one of us willing to lose face and back down. I felt a rush of pure, cold hatred.

I did not avert my gaze as the both the officers rose from their respective seats. I clenched my fists, seething with fury as at that moment, memories of yesterdays beating, the officers' taunting and images of Nikki all came tumbling through my mind.

The rage inside me bubbled over before I could rein it back. I glared at them, pouring every bit of hate and fury into that glare, as my frustration crystallised to rage, blind rage.

The moment of controlled anger seemed so unreal but yet

so prolonged. Everything I had dreamed of was gone and maybe the officers should have felt responsibility for reducing me to this?

I felt something snap inside me as I picked up my chair and hurled it at the encroaching officers. Unfortunately they managed to duck out of the way in time. They pressed the panic alarm, whose bells immediately reverberated throughout the police station, before they launched themselves at me, as if sprinters shooting from their starting blocks. I momentarily faltered, so before I had chance to brace myself for the oncoming attack I found myself being wrestled to the floor (I blame the cocktail of pills and booze for deadening my reflexes). I closed my eyes and winced in pain as my hair was yanked. One tug had brought me to a kneeling position and a couple more had me lying flat out on the floor. A violent struggle then ensued and I was struck several times until I was so winded and sore and my body so limp, that I found that I was incapable of defending myself. The breath flew from me, was literally sucked from my lungs, whilst pain cleaved through my chest. Wheezing, as I struggled for breath, I could offer no further resistance. Stinging sweat ran into my eyes, making me wince, whilst temporarily blinding me. I heard a sickening crunch of bone and felt one of the officers' knees in my back as my face was pushed hard into the floor, muffling my screams. I drew a breath that stung my nostrils as I felt the trickle of blood swim from my nose into my open mouth. It tasted slightly metallic but strangely comforting. It was something that I had tasted before, but for the moment, could not recall where and when. As the blood smeared my skin, I swallowed several times, sickeningly aware of the anguish beyond words. My legs were crossed and pinned and both my arms were twisted behind me, whilst my wrists were cuffed so tightly behind my back that I feared that they may snap. I felt myself wince as tears of pain sprung to my eyes.

God, you could tell that they were getting off on this and that it was a real adrenaline rush to them. I think that I even felt their erections pressing into me, but I was sure that they would later claim it to be their pepper sprays. The two exchanged a brief flurry of words with other officers that had just arrived at the scene, before I was grabbed under the arms and hauled to my feet.

Minutes later, now ensconced back in my holding cell and somewhat battered and bruised I found myself, yet again, being re-examined by the police doctor (if things carried on this way then I would be better off joining BUPA). I wished now that I had kept up the premiums on my health insurance.

Apparently there was nothing too amiss with me...just a bloody nose and light bruising to my ribs, back and wrists. The assault on me had already been written up as 'necessary force' and fully justified... apparently. I had opened my mouth to put my viewpoint across but then just snapped it shut. I could not summon the enthusiasm to argue the point as my soul and spirits were as crushed and bruised as my body, blinding pain piercing my skull.

Photographs of the injuries were taken, just in case I decided to lodge a complaint at a later date. I felt small and pathetic like a discarded doll and colder and lonelier than ever. My feelings were now a strange mixture of worthlessness, guilt and anger. My self-reproach was becoming destructive as my emotions stabbed within me like daggers, whilst in my mind's eye my life was falling down around me like a tower of cards caught in a strong breeze. My mind seemed unable to grasp at hope or to defend myself amid the inner howls of despair, fears slipping past the mental barriers that I had previously erected.

I began to question my own innocence and as hard as I tried, I could not remember my movements on the nights that I had earlier been questioned about.

Despite the interviewing officers now having confirmed with my general practitioner that I suffered with mental illness and clinical depression, they still believed that I was lying regarding my blackouts and my interpretation and recollection of events.

I only wished that I were, as the holes in my memory were bringing me to the brink of despair. I found myself even doubting my own sanity and righteousness.

I felt the eruption of renewed fear and felt sullied. How I now longed for the good news that would bring a bright fluttering to my dark and increasingly desolate soul.

After two days of relentless badgering and intimidation I was beginning to almost convince myself of my guilt. I felt hot with suppressed anger, but I could not think of anything to shift it. I wondered if I were destined to be tainted from cradle to grave.

Just as I was wallowing deep within the self-pity and self-loathing that had engulfed me, my train of thought was lost as the metallic clanking sound heralded the opening of the cell door.

I removed my head from my hands and glanced up at the entering figures. The custody sergeant's eyes met mine. It was strange but I was sure that I could sense disappointment in them.

He opened his mouth to speak but I quickly stepped in, my voice choked in rage.

"I have considered my options and I am ready to make a complaint now. I think two beatings in two days is slightly over egging the pudding, and I may not survive the third."

"OK. The taking of your statement, and if needs be, further photographs of the injuries can be arranged shortly. Someone from the complaints and discipline department and someone independent from the Police Complaints Authority will interview you. Matters such as these are taken very seriously these days."

"I am very glad to hear it."

As I spoke, I knew that I would enjoy taking revenge for my beatings. I waited for a response from either of the two officers in attendance but none was forthcoming.

My lips twitched as I swallowed but I said nothing further.

After what seemed like an eternity of muted unease, it was the custody sergeant who broke the deadlocked silence.

I had sensed the change in his mood instantly and saw him swallow, so I knew that words were coming.

"I will need you to come with us now."

I did not recognise his voice now due to its coldness and lack of feeling. I raised an enquiring eyebrow but received no explanation for our planned excursion, although I sensed that whatever was about to happen would not be good news for me. Now somewhat disillusioned, I did not verbalise my question as I wished to preserve at least a few more minutes with what little hope and dignity that I still had (although the scenario seemed ominous).

As the old saying goes 'what you don't know can't hurt you'.

I took a slow, cautious step forward before being grabbed by the arms. I was subsequently led from the cell with an officer each holding on to one of my arms…It made me feel like an invalid.

As the air crackled and popped around us, the tension electric, I was led down the corridor and up a short flight of stairs to the sergeant's desk. I heard whispers swelling into chatter, as ripples of movement caught my attention. As we turned the corner, I noticed that the interviewing officers were already stood there waiting, like hyenas biding their time before picking off the weakest of the herd.

I thought that I had spotted the cold glint of hunger and menace in their eyes, so I assumed that I was not about to receive any good news. I rolled my eyes in resignation and wondered what fate now awaited me. I was so pre-occupied with the officers' baleful stares that I failed to spot Diane stood alongside them at the desk.

It was just like a Friends Reunited reunion (and would undoubtedly turn out to be about as much fun).

I'd had such faith in Diane to begin with but she had proved to be a huge disappointment and as much use to me as a television in an Amish household.

I knew that I could only rely on myself from now on, and perhaps, with hindsight, it had always been that way.

As I approached the desk I felt all sets of eyes upon me. I felt my own eyes widen and my mouth fall open in a silent scream.

I averted my gaze but sensing the icy atmosphere I was certain that I would not be winning any popularity competitions. I let out a dramatic sigh as I tried to force myself to be calm. For a brief moment my mind shrank back from beyond the reach of my plight but my pulse would not slow down. I tried to look beyond the officers relentless, repetitive stares but all my foreboding thoughts were about to become a crashing reality as I was then informed that I was to be charged with the offences for which I was arrested. The custody sergeant began to read out the charges against me and asked if I had anything to say…

His voice was soft, but it sliced through me like a razor. It took me a second or two, to realize what he was saying. Once it had sunk in I could feel my eyes widen in horror but what could I have said, even if the words had not jammed in my throat?

The murder charge had echoed through the corridor and rebounded with an eerie stillness. To be charged with four counts of murder beggared belief, as I swallowed hard, I felt hollow and frail with panic. I was left utterly speechless; all that I could do was shake my head as my gaze travelled across all of their faces. The officers eyes flashed with triumph as fear and pain twisted through me. They left me dangling in silence.

I expected Diane to step in at any moment and say something but she also remained mute, with her eyes downcast as if the tiled floor held more interest to her than my current predicament.

Typical.

I shoved my hands into my pockets as I rocked on my heels. Blood pounded in my ears and I could feel my forehead crease into a deep frown. I groaned silently whilst momentarily squeezing my eyelids shut, as I could not believe Diane's absence of reaction.

I'd had such high hopes at the beginning that she would be able to get me released and the whole misunderstanding straightened out, but she had been so inconsequential that I doubted whether she could even organise a piss up in a brewery successfully. I groaned inwardly as I sensed the dream of freedom fading.

I felt like a child confronted with betrayal... Just why was it that everyone in my life, without fail, always let me down?

My thought process was snapped out of its rhythm as the custody sergeant then handed me a written copy of the charges and a date for my magistrate's court appearance. I felt my face collapse and fill with darkness-pits of damnation. A cold, damp darkness enveloped me and I shivered. I blinked and tried to clear my fogged brain, but was unsuccessful, so I tore my gaze away and just gave a brusque nod.

I learnt that I was not to be given bail and would instead be remanded in custody. I noted the officers' smiles of satisfaction indicating that the statement was sweet music to their ears.

I was still somewhat in a state of shock as I was led away to be fingerprinted and photographed. I blinked hard and tried to focus but my mind was in turmoil as I felt the raw terror bubble inside of me. I was not sure with the current developments as to whether I should be laughing or crying at the total absurdity of it all.

I assumed that the news of my arrest and now subsequently having being charged would spread like wildfire through the assorted press and media packs. I knew that my life would never be the same again, as I would be hounded day and night by the hostile press, even if found innocent. They would dig up scurrilous stories about me and 'friends' would cash in on my notoriety. I so knew that my 'Ex' would be at the head of the queue. To this day I still never knew why she had grown to hate me quite so much. I squeezed my eyes shut hoping to spark an answer. There seemed to be one lurking behind my thoughts, but it would not emerge into the light of my mind. As my sub-conscious bubbled, I once again experienced the bitter taste of pain and betrayal that had infected my life. Just as an image came to mind, my mind snapped back to reality as I found myself being escorted to a small room just around the corner, where I was asked to roll up the sleeves of my shirt. I was then instructed to dip my fingers into the inkpad and then press them onto a white card that was laid out on the desk in front of me. I had to do each finger individually with an officer rolling my digit across the card (the memories of finger painting as a kid came flooding back to me though I remembered it being far more fun than this).

My mind and thoughts began to drift although I was soon brought back to the grim reality of the situation by the attending officer roughly grabbing at my hand. I jumped with a start as he shot me an impatient look, jarring my memory. I swallowed.

On glaring up at the officer, I noted that as he ran the ink roller over both my hands, he appeared to be less than thrilled with his latest assignment. Once each handprint was inked to the officer's satisfaction it was preserved in exactly the same way as my fingerprints. I was informed that the set of distinct prints would now be stored on the police database.

George Orwell would be so proud that his foresight had

proven to be quite so accurate.

I was handed a couple of paper towels (my favourite) to wipe my hands with, but much like my solicitor, they proved ineffectual.

I would have been better off using white spirit or turpentine.

My hands were so badly stained that I would have qualified as an honorary member of 'the black hand gang'.

I then found myself being led away to be photographed.

I had not had this much excitement in ages, first finger painting and now happy snaps. It was like the Metropolitan Police's answer to Butlins.

I was photographed twice. Firstly face on and then to the side.

I was slightly peeved as it was not even my good side. I did not know why they bothered though as they could just as easily have used my passport photograph, as that already made me resemble one of Britain's most wanted criminals. I wondered if the police owned the franchise to passport photo booths as the outcomes were always spookily similar.

Once these formalities were done and dusted I was escorted back to the holding area, where I was asked more questions about my personal life but I did not respond to any of them.

Several glares flew my way but I ignored them. Having now been officially charged I was then informed that I was to be remanded in custody until the next court hearing.

I was informed that after being allowed to speak to my solicitor that I would be taken back to the holding cells to await transportation to the nearest prison.

My whole body shook as my mind froze.

A headache was forming behind my eyes as I knew the whole situation was crazy, insane, preposterous...

Moments later, I found myself being ushered into the interview room, where Diane and I were left alone. She looked straight at me and I knew exactly what she was thinking. I could sense that she eyed me differently now and seemed to be a little uneasy in my company. I resisted the temptation to shout, "BOO!", as I was sure that she would have jumped right out of her skin if I had of done. As I took my seat Diane offered me a cigarette, which I gratefully accepted. Upon lighting it, I inhaled deeply as my whole body sighed with relief at the kick of the now much needed nicotine fix. My voice sounded strained and a bit breathful, so I tried to relax and clear my mind of the negative thoughts that were currently bombarding my brain, as currently I felt rabid with fear and denial.

As I sat there reclining on the chair whilst blowing smoke rings towards the ceiling tiles, Diane went on to inform me that the police had now turned the case over to the Crown Prosecution Service, who would subsequently continue with the prosecution should they feel that there was enough evidence to proceed.

"The case will be heard by a magistrate, to whom the prosecution will disclose their evidence. The magistrate will most likely commit the case to a crown court. As you are probably aware Crown Court trials are conducted in front of a panel of jurors…"

As she spoke, my mind was cutting out so I was not absorbing all of her words.

I had frozen as my heart hammered within me. I still could not believe that I was to be charged with four counts of murder.

It was scandalous and just so hard to digest and to get my head around. As a remand prisoner, I was supposed to be innocent until proven guilty; although I suspected that it would not quite work out that way in reality.

As my mind snapped back to the interview room I found that Diane was still droning on, totally oblivious to the fact that I had temporarily drifted off into my own thoughts and consternations.

She went on to inform me that a barrister would be appointed to me and my counsel would attempt to make the jurors aware of my state of mind…

What exactly was that supposed to mean, was I supposed to reflect and repent?

I met her eyes and noted that she looked as tired as I felt, which in itself, was quite an achievement.

As Diane continued speaking, I was led to believe that before a trial date had been set at crown court I may need to make a number of appearances before at the magistrate's court, prior to committal proceedings.

It looked as though my social diary was going to be pretty full for the next few months. I supposed that I should have been grateful for these arranged outings as I did not get out too often these days. I wondered if I would be getting packed lunches.

Diane then went on to inform me that both she and my appointed barrister would need to prepare me for the stand.

God…I felt like Custer.

There also, apparently would be the preparation of a social inquiry report. The next bit of news hit me like a thunderbolt. Samantha was to be called as a witness for the prosecution but my, yet to be appointed, barrister would be able to cross examine her.

I shivered at the thought and found that I could not move, unable to believe my ears.

Diane carried on speaking but I was not taking in any of what she was saying. My mind could just not accept or wished to believe that Samantha would have betrayed my confidence in this way. I could not believe that she was to testify against me.

How could she?!

I was shocked by her betrayal and felt as if a sharp dagger had been thrust into my heart.

I felt my inner rage bubble again as I choked on my words but I tried to regain some composure with a quick intake of breath.

I just did not understand how Samantha could have done this to me, as I had trusted her implicitly. She knew all about my childhood abuse and trauma, my marital problems and subsequent breakdown, that accumulated in my attempted suicide and losing my job. I had told her about my past, my aspirations, my fears, my hopes and my insecurities, which I had never shared with anyone else, yet she had still chosen to betray me. I just could not understand why. I winced as the rage and hurt thundered through my temples, my head tightening again. I was mentally wiped out and could taste the bitterness I felt within me as I knew now that Samantha was just the same as all the others.

I should have known better than to trust anyone. I felt betrayed and the depth of that feeling surprised me. I had been

155

stung by betrayal previously and would not be making that fatal mistake again. I now walked the tightrope of emptiness as all my previous feelings for her had now been replaced with a cold calculated hatred. Such was life.

A moment of silence followed before Diane suggested that I ponder over my plea. I could plead 'not guilty' or I could enter a 'guilty' plea, on the grounds of diminished responsibility. For the moment, she appeared to have reached the same unvoiced conclusion that I had…namely, that the circumstantial and forensic evidence appeared to be insurmountable and that a jury may be heavily swayed by prior media coverage. Of course my motive and state of mind would have to be established, but as Diane continued to enunciate the possible forthcoming scenarios I felt my mind begin to drift again as I stared blindly around the room.

I had always had a short attention span, especially when I did not like the words I was hearing. I recognised that my options were fast disappearing. I felt profoundly shaken and inside as brittle as a New Labour election pledge. My anxiety and agitation were steadily rising, as if an oven thermometer as feelings of complete worthlessness and perhaps inappropriate guilt washed over me. My mind and body were frozen in trepidation of the impending scenario due to unfurl before me. I stared absently at the ceiling for several seconds before lowering my gaze.

Diane must have sensed that I had momentarily become disassociated with her dialogue as she had ceased speaking.

It took me a moment or two before I realised.

I eventually met her gaze.

"Sorry. I think my mind drifted off for a moment. This whole development has taken me by surprise a bit. I was expecting to be released with an apology, not beaten up on consecutive days and then charged with four counts of murder. What are they doing, clearing their books of all unsolved crimes? And as for Samantha betraying me…what can I say?"

My voice sounded tired as I let it trail away, although I suppose the hurt in my expression must have spoken volumes.

"I understand. A lot has happened to you in a very short space of time. Take time out to digest it all and to collect your thoughts. In the meantime, I will get the barrister up to speed regarding your circumstances thus far, but obviously they will need to converse with you in person before any court appearances. They will go through your account of events, (thoroughly, from beginning to end), prepare you for the stand, explain the proceedings that will occur and discuss with you your plea, and if relevant, any mitigating circumstances and state of mind."

Diane had not come out and directly stated it, but I now knew that she believed me to be guilty of the charges.

How the worm had turned.

I felt hot surges running through my body as I felt my panic and anxiety intensifying. I rubbed the back of my aching neck.

How I wished that I could leave all my childhood baggage and adult anger behind. The three decades of humiliation and hurt.

I felt utterly betrayed and itched to say something back to her but I could only think the words as my breath caught and I found that speech was momentarily impossible.

Obviously, I was too crushed, emotionally and mentally to speak. I could no longer handle the pressure and I felt as if a fist had penetrated my skull. I could only sit and stare vacantly at my hands which were clasped tightly whilst my thumbs absently circled like reeds caught in a strong breeze.

Seeming slightly unnerved Diane departed the interview room, allegedly to get the defence ball rolling (whatever that entailed) and promised to keep me updated with any developments later.

That was nice of her seeing as it was my life that hung in the balance. I had never been one to trust so there could be no response to the exasperation I felt. I was losing all illusion of control and sinking into madness. I had got burned again...sometimes I truly despaired.

The custody sergeant entered the room as Diane departed. I glared at them both but said nothing, before I was subsequently escorted back to the holding cell (after stopping briefly at the gentlemen's washroom to relieve my aching bladder).

Once safely ensconced back my cell I was brought some lunch, which consisted of fried chicken and chips and a can of fizzy orangeade, obviously from a nearby Kentucky Fried Chicken outlet. I wished now that I had known that this food option was available to me when I was brought the pigswill yesterday (or were it a case of the condemned man being given a final hearty meal)?

The food today smelled good enough to be delicious but I just picked at it as I could find no appetite now. I seemed to have lost all taste for food… as well as life.

My throat felt dry and gritty (as if I had fire in my lungs) so I pushed the meal aside and sat staring down absently at the concrete floor. I sensed the thin line between sanity and madness and wondered if I had yet crossed over its threshold, as I felt mentally numb and totally disconnected from the situation that I now found myself embroiled in. I felt so devoid of emotion that at this stage I may as well not have even been human. Uncontrollable flashes of memories and images from my past bombarded my senses and I felt as if a dark apparition had descended upon me, a palpable sense of evil. My mind was now racing and I felt totally unable to control the thoughts and processes of my mind, my visions driving me insane. The heart palpitations which I was now experiencing and the tightness in my head only added to the sense of total unease and restlessness that I now felt. Had I succumbed to the inevitable consequence of genetics and turned into my father? It was difficult to see how my life could get any worse. I was feeling totally disconnected, as though all of my emotions were being stripped away from me and that I was fast becoming just a hollow shell. I was almost becoming dizzy with thought as my mind raced uncontrollably, rabid with fear and denial. I knew that I could pass out or lose control at any given moment. I found myself bathed in sweat and trembling with fear so I sat down on the padded bench and pushed the pillow behind my aching back. I attempted to calm myself by taking deep breaths and attempting to block out the obsessive thoughts that were currently sucking the very essence from me. I felt as if I were in pure hell as I was feeling manic one moment and in the throws of depression the next, straining my already fragile condition. A nightmare world of inner visions swept down upon me and I could feel the grief oozing back, filling my brain. The severe headaches, sweating, nightmares, panic and fear were all adding to the cocktail of despair that I was now experiencing. I was cold and shivering, despite my Tee-shirt and shirt providing two layers of clothing. I just could not seem to get warm, even wrapping myself in the blanket did not seem to make a difference. My muscles and joints ached but I was not entirely sure as to whether or not that was due to the recent beating (sorry, justifiable force) or the icy chill of fear that I was now feeling run through my veins. I felt tired but I suppose that was to be expected. Despite this, however hard I tried to settle my mind I found that I had no control over my galloping thoughts. I began to doubt my own innocence and sanity, as I had no control over the blackouts which I experienced. The details were still too fuzzy in my mind but I longed to know for certain, even if that knowledge proved to be too terrible. I buried my head in my hands, as the questions bombarded my brain.

Had I really killed these women, and then blanked it out from my mind?

I felt all the more isolated.

Was I a monster?

Was this the depressing truth, which I was trying so hard not to accept?

Self-disgust washed over me, making me feel quite sick. As I dropped my head to my chest, all my fear and anxiety bubbled forth. It was awful to think of what I may have done. I felt overwhelming guilt and uncompromising remorse and I knew that I would be haunted for the rest of my life. I wished that I could remember, but my recollections were far from vivid as my brain exploded with panic whilst fear now held me firmly in its jaws, paralysing me. I laughed bitterly, almost snarling at the dark wings of guilt as remorse haunted me.

I knew that I could not survive a prison sentence as I felt sure that they would crucify me. Prison only represented the violence and horror from my childhood traumas, and I could not return to an environment such as that, as I would be back to square one.

My awareness lurched nervously as I knew that in a few weeks, or months, time I would plead 'not guilty' but that the jury would not find me so. The 'evidence' was too strong and the case had too much prior publicity for me to even begin to contemplate a fair trail. The verdict was inevitable.

I knew that I would be tried and declared guilty. The judge would denounce both myself, and my crimes, and I would be condemned and vituperated by the waiting public, media and assorted scavengers. I gasped for breath as the feelings welled up beyond my control and fed my own rage. I was more than aware that a lifetime of sadistic prison brutality would then await me. I felt a tingle of fear crawl up my spine, as my lungs tightened at the leap of panic. As I collected my thoughts a small part of me did not want to continue with the next course of action but I knew now that I had little choice. Everything seemed lost and my options were now totally exhausted, although if truth be known, I had relinquished that control a long time ago...

There must now be no more innocent deaths.

I tried to understand my crimes and what had led me to commit them, but the images and memories were still too vague and hazy in my mind's eye. I no longer knew what memories were real and what false memories the officers had now planted within me. I must have lost control and I swore to never let it happen again.

I was taking control of my own destiny as I could not take the risk of anyone else being harmed. The past was dragging me down like exhausted sleep and I was joining the ghosts.

I felt an overwhelming sense of guilt and remorse. Inside me there was nothing worthwhile left. I tried to think of a single reason to go on but everything I had ever cherished in my life had now been cruelly torn from my grasp. I knew that love was a lie, so I could not think of a solitary reason to go on with my miserable existence and the nightmare of living. There was nothing out there for me and I now feared the demons that dwelt within me. The black hole that I was now in just kept getting deeper and darker. There was only one way out. I knew that suicide would bring a quick end to my pain and release me from this dark feral world. It would be my only way to experience complete peace and sanctuary.

I felt as though I had little choice. I could not handle my own guilt... besides I had already lost everything.

I had no-one and I had nothing.

I knew that I was caught up in a web of lies and deceit but I was unsure as to whether it was of the police's making or my own.

I swallowed as if I could gulp down the thoughts but the small whisper inside my head was now a scream that I could no longer suppress. I knew how futile and worthless my life was and the rest of the world could go up in flames for all that I cared.

I had never known good fortune and I despised, with a vengeance, all the people who had driven me to this present moment in time.

Heaven and Hell, damnation and salvation, was there really any choice...or even any difference? My nerves jagged with the problem, the answer staying stubbornly out of reach.

Now came the problem of how to achieve my goal...

Reaching down to the tray I unwrapped the serviette which had come with the meal and removed the utensils. I began to slice and saw away at my wrists with the plastic knife, but that was barely scratching the surface of my skin. I fared no better with the plastic fork. I felt so physically numb that I could not even feel the implements slicing away at my flesh.

After a few minutes of miserable failure I abandoned that course of action and sought alternatives...

Picking up my bedding I attempted to tear the grey woollen blanket so that I could use it to hang myself, but the material was too strong (or I was too weak) for me to be able to rip it. How I now wished that I had not had my belt removed on arrival at the police station. With hindsight I now regretted that I had not pocketed the disposable razor that I had used to shave earlier in the day, as I felt sure that would have achieved the objective perfectly.

I was scared out of my wits but I still knew what needed to be done. I felt fear but I'd had to live with that fear everyday of my miserable existence. Any happiness that I had felt had only ever been transient. I felt so tired of life and now just longed for the tranquil peace of eternal sleep.

My inner restlessness was now so acute that it seemed suicide was the only answer. I knew that I did not want to be around (or was safe to be around) people anymore and my memory losses scared the hell out of me. Anyhow, I deserved to die as I had killed four innocent women, hadn't I? I felt ashamed as they'd had their whole lives ahead of them before I had cruelly and mercilessly snuffed them out. Rigid with trepidation, my heart fluttered inside my chest, the sensation unsettling. I knew that the general public and the throng of press and media packs would crucify me, so I could never return home even if freed.

Part of me just wished that I could remember the events more clearly, but the police had told me what had happened, what I had done to those poor innocent women, so some if not all, of the images were now cutting like razors through my mind.

I realised that my blackened soul was going to burn in the fires of hell for all of eternity... but I knew that I deserved it.

Nearly everyone must have unhappy childhood traumas, so I could not even use that as mitigation for my obscene and sickening behaviour. I knew that I was hopelessly out of control and that I needed stopping. I realised that I could no longer bear to look at myself in the mirror again. To reflect upon my raven black soul, the dark recesses in my psyche and to see those murdering eyes. I did not particularly want to live, not if I had killed those women, and besides I knew that I could not cope with life long incarceration. As I was now unable to function like a normal human being I did not want to feel anymore. Feeling was too painful an experience and there was only so much that I could withstand. Perhaps the worst crime of all was the crime of regret. Anyhow, I mused, I was already a prisoner of my own life. I hoped that I could achieve the ultimate freedom from the pain, fear and depression that had blighted my woeful existence. The events of the previous few days rolled back and I relived them all, so now a cold void sat where my dreams once lived and I could no longer separate my demons, which sat coiled as if waiting to pounce. Were they built on myth, my childhood nightmares or was I truly evil personified?

Why had all my dreams turned into nightmares and just who was responsible for that?

Guilt returned but I still felt the tendrils of doubt as I clenched my eyes shut in thought. I murmured wordless noises as I replayed the recent events through my mind again, hoping I suppose for a different outcome.

I knew that we all left this world as we had entered it, and as I had been for most of my life, alone.

Although I was becoming increasingly unsettled by what I was contemplating, I pushed the questions and doubts aside as I knew that there could be no more stalling…

I removed my shirt and Tee-Shirt and proceeded to tie them together, whilst twisting them as tightly as I could. I stood up upon the bench and leaning forward I attached them to the light fitting. I gave the clothing several sharp hard tugs, but thankfully the fitting did not come away. As I was of slight build, I felt comfortable that it would take my weight.

Excellent.

My hands were trembling as I moistened my ring finger with saliva and slipped the wedding band from my digit, whilst noting the irony of it now helping to do the job it all but started. I placed the band inside the twisted Tee-shirt. Leaning forward I then tied the entwined garments around my neck making sure that the knot was at the back of my neck and that I could feel the wedding band, although padded, at the front. I took a really deep breath as I hoped that I would not have the desire to breathe until long after I passed out, therefore not having to deal with the discomfort associated with laboured breathing. I remembered to keep my tongue out of my mouth as I had seen a film once where the hanged man bit his own tongue off, but went on to survive the hanging.

Neither was a prospect I wish to face.

I did not believe in the sanctity of life but I did believe in the will of the gods, so part of me was still waiting some form of divine inspiration. I should have known that it was not to be forthcoming.

I let out a bitter laugh.

I assumed that due to the constraints of moral precepts that I must have literally erased the memories of what had happened, as I truly had no vivid recollections of my murderous intent, and yet I was now more than certain that I had committed those truly evil deeds. I knew that my problems could not be fixed and that I had to bear the sense of responsibility. I felt exhaustion lower itself onto my shoulders. I uttered a silent prayer for forgiveness as relief mingled with the guilt…

I felt deserted and just hoped that the gods' mercy was infinite.

I felt a little apprehension, as I knew that my journey was now at an end, but I felt no fear, just lack of accomplishment as I realised that I was a complete failure. I was completely unfulfilled and alone in this wretched world and had failed to leave my mark in any way, shape or form. No-one had ever believed in me, so inevitably I was born to lose. At this thought my mood was suddenly shadowed by images and voices from my past as all of my relationships had been painful experiences and I knew that no-one cared about me or would mourn my passing when it came. Well, to hell with them all. I held no desire to savour their affliction as I had long since slammed shut the door to my soul and tasted the bitter end...

I knew that there was only one way to experience complete peace. The hell of my pointless life and existence had held absolutely no meaning and provided no valid reason to live; my guilt and its source were past. Nothing mattered anymore because deep pain was all that I could feel and it was daily becoming worse. I sensed that my spirit was sleeping somewhere cold and that I had been living a lie. I was truly a product of a broken home.

As if poised on the edge of darkness, I froze momentarily before I stepped off the bench. Tears welled up in my eyes and I began to cry softly as the tourniquet tightened around my neck. I felt the pleasure of pain. The ground swayed beneath me, but after a few seconds I felt my consciousness ebbing away and I was not hurting anymore as darkness swept in. The horrors had faded and the past had lost its grip on me. I had buried my heart and now I felt no pain, just freedom and serenity as ghostly images danced behind my eyes. I felt a sense of relief, as I knew that I did not belong in a world that was full of lies. Surely we were all saints and sinners, so I alone could not be held responsible (after all, I had only become a product of their hate).

As my mind drifted I envisioned paradise. I could picture myself in a darkened room, lit only by the flickering flames of scarlet votive candles, the eerie silence only being punctuated by the crackling of the open log fire and the occasional spluttering wax as a sudden chill breeze rakes through the room. As I turn to see the cause of the draught, Nikki glides in through the gaping doorway and melts into my outstretched welcoming arms.

Her eyes are lit with excitement and she purrs her contentment as I stroke her hair and trace the contours of her face with my fingers and then my lips.

The darkness had been swept away and I found that there was beauty in sadness. Now that I was feeling so anaesthetised I no longer felt the bitter sting of rejection or of wounded dignity. Knowing that Nikki and I would now be together I felt tranquil and at peace.

CHAPTER 15

REPERCUSSIONS

The peephole was snapped open and the custody sergeant peered into the cell.

"Oh fucking hell!"

His voice was booming and echoed around the adjacent corridors. Fellow officers alerted by the uproar were already responding to his cry long before his hand had slammed against the panic button. He fumbled on his chain for the correct key. On grasping it, he quickly inserted the key into the lock and turning the handle he flung the door open with such force that the thud of it hitting the wall resonated throughout the station. It was only interspersed by the clanging of the alarm bell and the footfalls of a dozen heavy police boots pounding along the corridors. The custody sergeant was in the process of cutting the immobile body down, when half a dozen uniformed officers appeared, wedging themselves into the doorway to the cell, seemingly too afraid or uncertain to enter.

They looked on at the custody sergeant fumbling with the ligature, noting that his face was pale and perspiring.

"For Christ sake, don't just stand there, give me a bloody hand, and one of you call the doctor and an ambulance immediately."

A damp chill filtered into the room.

He obviously could not live with the guilt of what he had done. Good riddance.

It is no great loss.

He deserved to die.

At least it will save the taxpayer the expense of paying for his keep whilst he was to be banged up.

None of those opinions were aired verbally but the custody sergeant knew what the officers were thinking to themselves, as he was thinking exactly the same. He hated himself for that thought. He used to be a good man... a humanitarian. He had joined the police force as he wanted to serve and help the local community and to make a difference to people's quality of life.

What had happened to him? Why had he become so cynical?

Perhaps it was inevitable that the reality of modern life (and the dregs of society that he had shared his last two decades with) had long since eroded his previous good intentions?

While he mused, he had managed to loosen the ligature and had dragged the motionless body down. He laid it onto the floor and rolled the prisoner onto his back, seemingly making sure that the body did not twist, although the officers that were looking on were not entirely sure what difference it would make, as the prisoner looked like a goner to them.

The custody sergeant then dropped down beside him, fingers going to his throat checking for a pulse. He appeared not to find one, and the officers were secretly pleased…well, murdering scumbag deserved it didn't he? They could not fail to notice that the sergeant's face was ashen as they witnessed a bead of perspiration drip from his forehead onto the prisoner's outstretched but motionless body.

"There is no pulse, but the body is still warm. Get the bloody doctor here now…and where is that fucking ambulance?"

Fortunately they did not operate a swear box policy at the station.

The officers watched avidly as the custody officer then knelt beside the shoulder of the prone body. They assumed that he was now desperately trying to recall his first aid training as he paused momentarily (eyes closing) as if trying to remember what he was supposed to do next.

As the assembled officers looked on, they saw that the sergeant began by opening the prisoner's mouth and appeared to look into his throat, presumably to ensure that the airway was clear.

The custody sergeant had taken a deep breath before commencing the resuscitation procedure. God… how he hoped that the prisoner had not bitten off his own tongue. Thankfully the prisoner had not so he then proceeded by tilting the prisoner's head back slightly to open the airway. He put upward pressure on the jaw to pull it forward. He swallowed hard, and silently prayed to whatever gods would answer him, that he was doing the procedure correctly, whilst the assembled uniformed officers thanked the heavens that it was not one of them that had to do this.

The sergeant then proceeded by pinching the prisoner's nostrils closed with his thumb and forefinger. He then placed his mouth tightly over the prisoner's. He gestured sharply in disgust, but no mouthpiece had been forthcoming and neither the doctor or ambulance crew had yet arrived at the scene. He paused for a brief moment, obviously suddenly concerned that the prisoner could have something contagious that he may pass on to him.

The assembled officers supposed that the sergeant had a point, as in this day and age you could not be too careful, and it was always best to err on the side of caution. They certainly would not have proceeded without one, not for that murdering bastard, that was for damned sure.

The custody sergeant felt a tad uneasy but knew that he had no choice really but to continue. He blew two quick breaths and leaned back to see if the prisoner's chest rose. It did not.

How the assorted officers wished that they could tap into the sergeant's thoughts, as he appeared to have the weight and worries of the world upon his shoulders at present.

If they had of been able to, they would have known that he was still whispering a desperate prayer to any god that would listen.

He knew full well that he would be dragged over the coals for the turn of events. First the alleged assaults on a prisoner, supposedly under his supervision, and now this suicide attempt. It never rained but it poured. He was the custody officer so knew that the buck would ultimately stop with him.

Oh Christ, there would be a full-scale enquiry regarding the confusion of events. He would probably be suspended, and could even lose his job. His wife would be livid, and how on earth would he manage the mortgage repayments? He knew that the prisoner's survival was now inextricably entangled with his own future within the force and his continued quality of life. Moments of exasperation, impatience and resentment coursed through him in equal measures, as he felt a twinge of tension.

"Breathe goddammit."

He released the prisoner's nostrils and looked for the chest to fall as he exhaled.

Although the small crowd of officers that had now gathered remained, there fell a hushed silence over the proceedings.

You could have heard the proverbial pin drop.

The custody sergeant again listened for the sounds of the prisoners breathing, but could hear nothing. He then leaned forward in an attempt to try and feel breath on his cheek, but he felt none. Gripped by panic and now fearing the worst, he began agitatedly repeating the procedure.

How he now wished that he had phoned in sick today.

Just at that moment the doctor rushed in and knelt down level with the prisoner's shoulders. The sergeant briefly explained the situation and his prior actions before stepping aside to allow the doctor some room to work. As he stepped back he went silent in what might have been sadness or disbelief, whilst involuntarily crossing his fingers behind his back. As the custody sergeant had been bringing him up to speed, the doctor was continuing with the same procedure that he himself had just ceased.

There was still no sound of breathing or any chest movement, so fearing that the prisoner's jaw may be damaged he held the prisoner's lips closed and blew into his nose. He allowed the air to escape by removing his mouth and separating the prisoner's lips. He then, maintaining the airway, and using his hand placed on the prisoner's forehead, gently pinched the patient's nose closed.

The assembled officers looked on intently as the doctor then proceeded to take a long deep breath and placed his mouth, in an airtight seal, around the prisoners' mouth. He gave two full breaths (lasting a few seconds each), taking a breath between them, whilst still watching for the prisoners chest to rise and fall.

He listened and then felt for air escaping during exhalation.

"Does anyone know the expected time of arrival for the ambulance?"

The response from the observing officers was almost in unison.

"Apparently, they will be here any minute."

The doctor's voice was tense and his expression was one of

irritation and perplexity, "Well that had better be the case as we are close to losing him… If we have not already."

As a murmur ran round the cell, the doctor continued with his resuscitation procedure. Again, the chest did not rise, so he repositioned the prisoner's head slightly further back and repeated the breaths.

The custody sergeant uttered a silent prayer as he looked on at the doctor's movements…

(God, he seemed rough and heavy-handed for a medical man and he instantly felt a wave of pity for the doctor's wife).

Still nothing, the patient had remained immobile throughout.

He watched the doctor work intently and caught his expression that seemed to be masked with anxiety and foreboding.

The doctor had now repositioned himself so that he now sat astride the prisoner's thighs. The officers continued watching from the sidelines as he then placed the heel of one of his hands against the prisoner's abdomen, slightly above the navel. He placed his other hand on top of the first. He pressed down into the abdomen with a quick forward and upward thrust. He continued by giving several steady thrusts. He worked frantically and with purpose although inside he was beginning to suspect that it might be a forlorn hope. He therefore felt immensely relieved when the paramedics and ambulance crew, bedecked in their reflective jackets, came bursting in through the door and took over.

His breath hung in the air like invisible whispers as he thanked the gods that the cavalry had arrived.

CHAPTER 16

D. O. A

The hospital administrator stood before the assorted throng of press and media who were eagerly awaiting the release of what would be a very short press statement. His hand absently ran through his steel grey hair as glare from the lighting rig and flash photography stung his eyes. Slightly squinting he raised his fist to his mouth and cleared the frog from his throat before speaking.

"At 5pm today, Mr Jamie Allen was pronounced dead. Upon admittance into the hospitals emergency department it was established that he had absent respirations and absent heart beat. Due to pulmonary complications there was, unfortunately, nothing that we could do to save him.

His family have come forward and subsequently been notified…"

A barrage of questions from the assembled reporters assaulted his senses, but they were left unanswered.

"I have nothing further to add, thank you, gentlemen."

With that he turned on his heels and headed back to his air-conditioned office. As he did so he hoped that his wife had remembered to set the video recorder as he had specifically instructed her to do. It would be good to watch himself on the television later tonight, and undoubtedly his mum would be mightily proud of him. He just hoped that he had appeared articulate and professional and not like a teacher just pretending to be interested.

Maybe Andy Warhol was right when he said that everyone would be famous for fifteen minutes?

EPILOGUE

As Diane was approaching her driveway she heard the unmistakeable ring tone of her mobile phone. Being careful not to spill the files that she had wedged under her arm, she began rummaging into her shoulder bag. She grabbed the phone and flipped it open to speak.

"Hello... Oh my god, are you kidding?

Her voice crackled with bewilderment as the grip on her mobile phone unconsciously tightened.

"What, it has just been announced? Oh God, I was just dropping some case files off at home and grabbing a quick shower before intending to shoot back up to the police station. This is terrible. Even if he did all those terrible things, of which I still have my doubts, he did not deserve that. He needed help. Do you know if his family have been traced and informed? Oh. Right, look I am almost home. Let me get inside and I will ring you back from the home phone as you are breaking up on this one. I will only me a few minutes. OK, bye."

She clicked the clam phone closed and dropped it back into her shoulder bag. Her mind was numb, still suffering from the shock of the news. She could not help but to think that it all could have been so avoidable. Why on earth was he not on a suicide watch? He was taking prescribed anti-depressants for Christ sake, surely the Metropolitan Police's finest would have sussed that he may be a little down?!

It truly was a sad and tragic case and a mixture of anger and sadness overtook the numbness that she felt inside of her.

She had reached her gate and swinging it open, crunched up the gravel drive (that was currently splintered with sunlight) to the porch. She really needed to cut back some of the bushes and shrubbery, as it was getting terribly overgrown and her front bay window was almost buried behind a tangled screen of rose bushes.

She could not wait to hit the shower and wash the stains of the day from her body. Just a quick call to the office first and then the warm jets of water could work their magic on her tense and aching muscles.

She fumbled inside her handbag for her front door keys and eventually retrieved them, taking care not to spill the case files that were still carefully wedged firmly under her arm. She slid the key into the lock and gently nudged the door open, keeping it ajar with her foot as she bent down to place the files onto the wooden hall table. She then stooped to gather the post and the milk from the doorstep. As she did so, self-analysis absorbed her. She was inwardly pondering as to whether or not she could or should have done more to help her client. Had she been as equally culpable as the police, for his loss of life?

Her train of thought was disturbed as she heard a heavy footfall and saw a dark shadow fall across her. She went to look up but as she did so she felt a gloved hand clasped her mouth tightly shut. She could taste the beaten leather, and at that moment she saw the glint of steel as a knife flashed across her eye line. She froze in terror as she was bundled through the open door and into the hallway. She heard the foreboding sound of the front door click shut behind them. She knew what awaited her.

Before she had time to cry out for help or plead for mercy, she heard the knife click shut as she felt his hands clamp tightly around her neck. She gasped for air, whilst kicking out desperately, her hands flailing wildly, trying to scratch and claw at her assailant. It was all to be to no avail, as she felt herself becoming weaker as her assailant grew stronger. She noted that her breath was becoming weak and rasping as pain ripped the air from her lungs and everything went black for a split second. As her hands flew to her throat she felt her strength and life cruelly ebbing away from her. Her eyes were bright with tears as a galaxy of dust hung suspended in the air above her, having been disturbed by the struggling and twisted forms below. Her face squeezed tight with pain. He was just too strong and too powerful to fight off and the tears were now streaming down her face, coating her lips with the taste of salt before dropping off of her chin on to the carpet below.

Although she could not see his face she could feel his cold hateful stare on the back of her neck. She convulsed in one final shudder as her hair fell forward in a snarled mess. She had long since resigned herself to her fate before all light was extinguished and the silence and darkness had closed in around her...